J. T. EDSON'S
FLOATING OUTFIT

The toughest bunch of Rebels that ever lost a war, they fought for the South, and then for Texas, as the legendary Floating Outfit of "Ole Devil" Hardin's O.D. Connected ranch.

MARK COUNTER was the best-dressed man in the West: always dressed fit-to-kill. **BELLE BOYD** was as deadly as she was beautiful, with a "Manhattan" model Colt tucked under her long skirts. **THE YSABEL KID** was Comanche fast and Texas tough. And the most famous of them all was **DUSTY FOG**, the ex-cavalryman known as the Rio Hondo Gun Wizard.

J. T. Edson has captured all the excitement and adventure of the raw frontier in this magnificent Western series. Turn the page for a complete list of Berkley Floating Outfit titles.

J.T. Edson

UNDER THE STARS AND BARS

BERKLEY BOOKS, NEW YORK

For William R. Hicks of Portsmouth,
Hants, who lets his dad read my books.

The sudden drumming of hooves mingling with the crackle of revolvers' shots, accompanied by a ringing shout of "Yeeah! Texas Light!". Following them, smoke and flames might rise from a Quartermasters' Corps depot; a supply train would be found, its wagons wrecked, their loads carried off and teams driven away; a cursing Artillery officer could find the guns in his battery spiked and his magazine exploded.

That was how the men who rode under the Stars and Bars flag of the Confederate States fought against the Yankees in Arkansas. One name ranked high when such incidents were mentioned. That of an eighteen year old captain, the commanding officer of the Texas Light Cavalry's Company "C".

His name was Dusty Fog.

PART ONE

The Scout

"Here they come now, Captain Fog," whispered Logan Huntspill, head of the Confederate States' spy-ring which operated out of Pine Bluff and maintained a watch over the activities of the Union's Army of Arkansas along the Arkansas River south of that town. "What do you reckon to them?"

Keeping his field-glasses to his eyes, Captain Dustine Edward Marsden Fog turned his attention from the original objects of his scrutiny. Big, piggish of face, his almost bloated fat body straining the gold-lace-trimmed blue uniform's seams, General Buller stood with several of his senior officers on top of a small knoll about half a mile from the two Rebels' position. The Yankees were looking or pointing across the Arkansas River to where a small, derelict steamboat bobbed at its moorings by the eastern bank. Beyond the old side-wheeler sat a cluster of dilapidated log cabins. Neither the boat nor the buildings seemed to merit

3

the attention lavished on them by Buller's party.

A sense of expectancy bit into Dusty as he turned his glasses in the direction indicated by his companion. At least he was going to see the reason for his being given orders at Prescott to ride as fast as possible to Pine Bluff and contact Huntspill.

Focussing the glasses on the new subject, Dusty felt both puzzled and a sense of anti-climax. The tall, thickset, bearded man sharing the concealment of the large clump of buffalo-berry bushes with him had hinted that something of great importance was due to happen. According to Huntspill's message, brought by a courier to General Jackson Baines Hardin's headquarters at Prescott, the Yankees were shortly to receive some new form of weapon that might once again put them on the offensive in the Toothpick State.

According to Ole Devil Hardin, Huntspill had always been accurate with his news and was no alarmist. The spy had stressed the extreme urgency of the matter and requested that an officer be sent to help him assess the extent of the danger. That had been sufficient to cause the commanding general of the Confederate States' Army of Arkansas and North Texas to respond immediately. So Dusty was expecting to be confronted by a sight of more apparent importance than met his gaze. Especially after crossing the Ouachita River—the boundary separating the two opposing armies—and riding nearly sixty miles through enemy-held territory in just over twenty-four hours.

Going by his tone and expression, Huntspill felt doubts as to whether the officer sent by Ole Devil would have an opinion worth hearing. Of course, he remembered how Dusty Fog had been promoted to captain in the field after his superior officer had been killed and he had led Company "C" of the Texas Light Cavalry in the charge that had turned the course of the battle at Mark's Mill to the South's favour. In meetings with other members of that regiment, Huntspill had heard his companions' name mentioned several times; but he had formed an entirely different impression of what Captain Fog would be like.

The Texans had told of Dusty's lightning fast withdrawal of his two revolvers and superlative accuracy when shooting from either hand. Never modest about the prowess of their State's favourite sons, the beef-heads had claimed that Dusty Fog was the equal of Turner Ashby or even the Grey Ghost, John Singleton Mosby, as a military raider. A further boast—clearly false, even if the other two be true—was that Dusty possessed the bare-hand fighting knowledge to let him lick any man on the Confederate or Union side of the civil conflict.

Captain Fog had proved to be something of a disappointment to Huntspill. A young eighteen, he had a handsome, though not strikingly so, face with intelligence in its lines and grey eyes that looked at a man steadily. In height he would stand no more than five foot six inches; but with the wide shoulders and lean waist that hinted at considerable strength. A regulation white Jefferson Davis campaign hat was thrust back on his curly, dusty-blond hair. In the front centre of its crown rode a badge formed of a five-pointed star, with the letters TLC on it, in a laurel-wreath decorated circle. Based on the Lone Star State's coat-of-arms, that was the insignia of the Texas Light Cavalry.

Possibly being Old Devil Hardin's favourite nephew gave Dusty certain privileges. Certainly he flouted the Confederate States' Army's *Manual of Dress Regulations* on several points in his uniform.

The boots and tight-legged, yellow-striped riding breeches conformed with *Regulations*. Although his cadet-grey tunic had two rows of seven buttons on its double-

breast, and a stand-up collar bearing the triple
three-inch-long, half-inch-wide gold bars—the highest still
looking newer than its mates—denoting his rank, it lacked
the prescribed *"skirt extending halfway between hip and
knee."* True, its sleeves carried the decorative double-
strand gold-braid Austrian knot "chicken guts," as a further
aid to marking him as a captain, above their cavalry-yellow
cuffs. However, the required black silk cravat was replaced
by a tight-rolled scarlet bandana of the same material, long
ends trailing down the front of his tunic.

About his lean waist was suspended a definitely non-
issue gunbelt which possessed no means of carrying a
sabre. Instead it had two holsters carefully designed so as
to permit him to draw the matched bone-handled 1860
Army Colts with the minimum of effort and in the shortest
possible time. The long-barrelled revolvers' butts pointed
forwards, but seemed to be angled differently than the conventional Army mode of carriage. Like many of the Texans
Huntspill had met, Dusty tied the tips of his holsters down
with pigging thongs knotted around his thighs.

While the small captain looked neat, despite the long,
hard ride, he did not strike Huntspill as having the experience necessary to judge the potential of the Yankees' secret
weapon—whatever it might be.

Sensing his companion's feelings, Dusty ignored them.
He had long since grown accustomed to strangers' reactions to his lack of height and had developed skills which
more than off-set it. Contrary to Huntspill's thoughts, he
did possess a remarkable talent for unarmed combat. In
addition to being able to handle his fists in the conventional
manner, he had gained a thorough working knowledge of
jujitsu and *karate*—all but unknown at that time in the
Western Hemisphere—from his Uncle Devil's Japanese
valet. Having solid, hard-earned achievements behind him

already, and backed by a good, practical education, Dusty could shrug off other people's lack of confidence when it was caused by misgivings on account of his height.

Although Dusty would later come into contact with two very prominent members of the Confederate States' Secret Service—rescuing Rose Greenhow single-handed from a Yankee prison* and sharing two dangerous missions† with Belle Boyd, the Rebel Spy‡—this was his first contact with one of that organisation. He had been impressed by Huntspill's efficiency, satisfied with the arrangements made for them to be undetected while watching the Yankees, but could not help wondering if the spy had acted hastily in requesting a second opinion on what was, ostensibly, a straightforward matter.

Of course, the presence of General Buller hinted that something extra special might be in the air. The current commanding general of the Union's Army of Arkansas had never been noted for taking an active participation in the affairs of his soldiers. So Dusty searched the objects of Huntspill's interest for some hint of their importance.

Riding parallel to and about a quarter of a mile from the west bank of the river came what appeared to be an ordinary troop of Federal Cavalry in columns of four. They wore the peaked fatigue kepi, tunic, riding breeches and boots that were fast becoming the standard uniform for the Union Army's mounted troops. Each man carried a revolver butt-forward in a close-topped holster on the right of his belt and had a sabre suspended from the slings at its left. Well-mounted, good riders, they might be a better class of soldier than one usually saw in the Yankees' Army

* Told in *Kill Dusty Fog!*

† Told in *The Colt and the Sabre* and *The Rebel Spy*.

‡ More of Belle Boyd's story is told in *The Bloody Border, Back to the Bloody Border, The Hooded Riders* and *The Bad Bunch*.

of Arkansas; but they hardly seemed to warrant exceptional concern or urgency.

Or did they?

Certain significant factors began to strike Dusty. Directing his glasses at the nearest rider, he studied the insignia on the front of the kepi. It was not the usual flattened "X" made by two sabres, but a pair of crossed cannon above which a silver number "14" was superimposed with the letter "A." Given that much of a clue, Dusty examined the colour of the tunic's facings and the stripe along the seam of the breeches' leg. They were scarlet instead of the expected yellow.

"Well I'll be——!" Dusty began, lowering the glasses and turning to Huntspill. "They're artillery, not cavalry."

"That's what I figure when I saw them arrive," the spy answered. "Only they don't have any guns along. They rode in yesterday just like you're seeing them now. Had three battery-wagons and a travelling forge, but nary a cannon."

"Could've had them in the wagons, maybe?"

"I don't reckon so. Three wagons wouldn't carry all their gear and enough cannons for that many men to be needed."

"Mountain howitzers aren't all that big," Dusty pointed out. "Except that those fellers don't even have them along. Could be the Yankees've run short of cavalrymen and're using some of the culls from their artillery to make up the numbers. Only those fellers don't look nor ride like throwouts from any outfit."

"They sure don't," agreed Huntspill, knowing "culls" to be the poorer stock cut out as useless from a cattle-herd. "Anyways, if what I've picked up is true, these fellers're mighty special. That's why I sent word for Ole——"

Then the burly civilian realised that Dusty had swivelled

the field-glasses upwards again.

"Did they have those stove-pipes hanging on their saddles?" Dusty interrupted, staring at the riders.

"Huh?" grunted Huntspill, whipping his own glasses to his eyes.

From his position among the bushes the spy could see some of the fifteen men in the column nearest to the river. Each had what looked like a five-foot length of three-inch stove-pipe dangling from the fork of his McClellan saddle. Not just an ordinary piece of pipe, however. The lower end had been cut in half to form a trough about twelve inches long. A pair of metal bands encircled the tube, the upper having a steel rod fixed to either side of it and arranged so they could be swivelled and locked in any position from horizontal—as at the moment—to vertical. Based on the lower band and pointing upwards along the top of the tube was what looked like an elongated rear leaf-sight for a rifle.

"No," Huntspill admitted. "They didn't have them on their saddles yesterday."

"Or them pouches on the backs of their saddles?" Dusty went on.

"Can't say I noticed them either," the spy confessed.

Having always earned his living as a riverboat man, a fact shown by his nautical peaked cap and clothing, Huntspill could be excused for failing to see anything out of the ordinary about the horses' equipment. Born and raised in a land where a horse was an essential part of life, rather than a mere means of transport, Dusty had recognised that the pouches were not usual Federal Army accoutrements. Attached to the rear of the saddle, they consisted of four leather tubes slightly less than two feet long hanging on either flank.

"Action left!" bawled the major leading the party, as

they came level with the boat and cabins. "Five hundred yards. Five degrees elevation. Incendiary, then high explosive. Prepare to fire!"

"What the hell——?" Huntspill began, watching the four lines halt at the major's first words.

Working with the swift, trained orderliness that told of long practice, the men dismounted. Immediately, without waiting for further instructions, the soldiers of the right side column took the reins of the other horses in their own section of four. While the second and third member of each section peeled the saddle-pouches from their mounts, the man nearest to the river unstrapped his tube from its position and cradled it in his arms.

"So that's it!" Dusty breathed, giving his attention to the forward section.

"What?" demanded Huntspill, staring at the scene of orderly confusion with an expression of incomprehension.

Letting the question go unanswered, Dusty watched the four Yankee artillerymen. Carrying his tube, the first moved away from the horses. Resting the end of the trough on the ground, he turned downwards the two steel rods and spiked their tips into the soil. After making an adjustment to the angle at which the tube was pointing, he raised and set the leaf sight on the rear band.

Resting his pouches on the ground, the second man opened the lid of a tube. From it he drew a metal cylinder about eighteen inches long, with a short truncated cone at one end and a sharp spike on the other.

"What the hell is that thing?" Huntspill hissed.

"A Hale Spin-Stabilised rocket," Dusty explained. "And some kind of gun for sending it in the right direction."

"Where's the stick?" asked the spy. "All the rockets I ever saw had one."

"Not this kind," Dusty replied. "I've read and heard

about them. It's got three curved metal vanes at the blunt end where the gas that makes it go blows out. Seems they make the rocket spin like a rifle bullet and keep it flying straight."

While they had been talking, the soldier had placed the rocket on to the trough and inserted the sharp nose up the tube. Stepping aside, he made way for the first man. After connecting a lanyard to the ring of the rocket's friction-primer, the first Yankee rested his foot on the lower end of the tube.

Turning his glasses, Dusty saw that all fifteen launchers had been set up and were loaded ready for use. No regular form of artillery could have been prepared in so short a time. Then he resumed his watch on the first section.

"Fire!" roared the battery commander.

A sharp tug on the lanyard caused the serrated iron ignition-bar to scrape across and set into operation the highly-combustible priming compound. A spark of flame stabbed among the propellant charge. The slow-burning mixture of nitre, sulphur and charcoal, forced under great pressure into the 3¼-inch light iron case, took fire and began to emit its gas.

With a spurt of flame and sudden "whoosh!," the rocket disappeared up the tube, burst from the muzzle and streaked across the river. It flew true, making for the side of the boat. Watching its flight, Dusty saw it strike the wall of the side-wheel's cabin and understood the reason for the sharp point. Instead of bouncing back, the rocket spiked into the timber and held there. Rupturing under the impact, the case allowed a flow of blazing "Greek fire" mixture to pour on to the wood.

The other fourteen rockets made their curving flight across the Arkansas River. Three more stuck into the boat and the remainder landed on, or between, the log cabins.

Red glows of flame licked upwards, dancing over the sun-dried timbers.

Holding a rocket, the third man of the section advanced. Dusty saw that the missile's head was more cone-shaped than pointed. Again the reloading process was faster than any cannon could be charged. Fifteen hands tugged on lanyards and the rockets spun through the air towards their targets. On striking, the reason for the differently-shaped heads became apparent. Instead of spreading "Greek fire," the second broadside's rockets exploded on impact.

"Whooee!" Dusty breathed, lowering his glasses. "Wasn't *that* something?"

"I've never seen anything like it!" Huntspill replied, glaring as if mesmerised at the flames consuming the old side-wheeler.

"I'd heard the Hale's were an improvement on the old Congreve stick-stabilised rockets Jeb Stuart used one time," Dusty drawled. "But I didn't know they were this effective."

"They're deadly, huh?"

"Deadly enough. Only there's more to it than just that."

"How do you mean, Captain?"

"Surprise," Dusty elaborated. "You mind what we thought when we first saw those jaspers riding up?"

"That they were an ordinary cavalry patrol," Huntspill replied.

"Sure," Dusty said soberly. "Take it this way. Some of our fellers see that battery riding along between five hundred yards and a mile away across the Ouachita or the Caddo. They reckon it's just a bunch of Yankee fly-slicers out for a ride. Then they cut loose with those rockets. Either incendiary or high-explosive'd do. It'd throw our boys into confusion. If an attack was launched straight after that, with our folk set back on their heels and wondering what the hell's hit them, it'd have a better than fair chance of succeeding."

Which just about confirmed Huntspill's summation of the situation. He looked at the small, soft-spoken, almost insignificant young man by his side and was suddenly aware of Dusty's strength of personality. That was no bald-faced stripling, placed in a position of trust through family influence, but a shrewd, discerning cavalry officer.

"What're you figuring on doing, Captain Fog?" the spy asked, in a far more respectful tone than he had shown up to that moment.

"I'm going to spread the word to our people," Dusty replied.

"We can't be sure where the Yankees'll hit with those blasted rockets," Huntspill protested.

"Then we'll have to guess. Likely they'll go for the targets that'll do most damage first, before word gets out what they're at."

"That's likely enough. What do *you* reckon it'll be?"

"There's three comes to mind," Dusty replied, looking pointedly at the burning sidewheeler. "Uncle Devil's navy."

"Those three 'tin-clads' on the Ouachita?" grinned Huntspill, with the cheerful contempt of a man who had handled the helm of a fast boat that ran along the Arkansas and Mississippi Rivers.

"They might not be Big Muddy mail packets, but they've got four Williams rapid-fire cannon and two twelve-pounder boat-howitzers mounted on each of 'em," Dusty pointed out. "Which they've done a whole heap to help stop the Yankees crossing the Ouachita."

"I'm not gainsaying it," the spy said, thinking of the trio of small, lightly armoured—hence the name "tin-" instead of "iron-clad"—steamboats. Their shallow draught, no more than two feet, made them useful vessels along the winding, narrow waters of the Ouachita River. "Trouble being we don't know which the battery'll try for first."

"That's soon settled," Dusty stated. "We'll warn all three."

"We——?"

"Me and my men."

"There're only three of you," Huntspill reminded Dusty.

"Why sure," the small Texan agreed. "Your message said come fast and you can't do *that* at Company strength. So I just brought along a couple of my men in case you needed them."

"Then how——?" the spy began.

"The *Georgia* works south out of Camden," Dusty explained. "I'll send Kiowa there with the word. The *Texarkana* patrols between Camden and Vaden, up in Clark County, and the *Skimmer* runs between Vaden and Arkadelphia. So I'll tell Vern Hassle to cut across to Arkadelphia and call in at Vaden on my way to tell Uncle Devil about the rocket battery. It won't take me far out of my way."

No matter how he looked at the matter, Huntspill could not find fault with Dusty's arrangements. Earlier, the spy might have doubted the youngster's ability to make the return journey unescorted. Such a doubt now never entered his head. He guessed that the Texan had called the play correctly. Certainly the rocket battery's most profitable targets would be the destruction of the "tin-clads." Their exposed engines and boilers made them particularly susceptible to an incendiary bombardment. With them out of action, a crossing of the Ouachita River would be much easier and safer than while they remained afloat.

On top of that, Huntspill knew there was no faster

means of spreading the warning about the battery. Even if
the boats should be on patrol when the Texans arrived, a
message could be left for their captains. Each of the river-
side towns had a telegraph station, permitting the news to
be spread along its wires.

"We'd best get going," the spy suggested. "I'll see if I
can learn where the battery's headed and get word there.
Good luck to you, Captain Fog."

"And to you," Dusty replied. "If I get caught, I'll be
sent to a prison camp. If they get you, you'll be shot."

"It's a chance I have to take," Huntspill said and led the
way back through the bushes. Behind them, the battery's
personnel were packing up their gear at the end of the demonstration.

Between Dusty's thighs, the large, spirited black stallion moved easily in a diagonal two-beat gait. First its off
fore and near hind feet struck the ground, then the near
fore and off hind, carrying its rider in a fast, mile-consum-
ing, but energy-preserving trot. Highly-skilled in all matters equine, Dusty held several views which were almost
tantamount to heresy in that day and age. His demands on
the shoeing of horses had led to considerable heated con-
troversy in the Texas Light Cavalry,* but not as much as
had his insistence that every member of Company "C"
learn how to "post" when travelling at a trot. Little used at
that period in Texas, regarded with suspicion or as cissified
almost, it said much for the strength of Dusty's control
over them that the hard-bitten, hard-riding, harder-fighting
men of Company "C" had acceded to his point of view.
They had discovered that they and their mounts benefited

---

* These demands are explained in *The Fast Gun*.

from "posting" and ignored the comments of the unenlightened; or answered the more opprobrious criticism with two-fisted arguments.

Supporting himself with the balls of his feet in the stirrup-irons and by the bony structure rather than the fleshy pads of his buttocks, Dusty inclined his shoulders a few inches before his hips. He sat far enough forward on the low-horned, double-girthed† range saddle so that his weight was directly over the vertical stirrup leathers. Keeping his hip joints straight, he used his knees as the pivotal points. Automatically he rose and sank from the saddle in time with the stallion's movements. The long-gaited black moved with plenty of spring and action, causing Dusty to rise high but without conscious effort or suffering inconvenience from the motion.

When it was carried out correctly, the combination of an alert, expert rider and a well-trained, healthy horse could post at a fast trot for many miles without undue fatigue to man or mount. Dusty had mastered the art and, being light of weight, gained the best out of the seventeen-hand stallion; one of a trio he had selected, broken and trained for his own use.

How effective posting the trot could be showed in the fact that, leaving the spy shortly before midday, he had dispatched his two men and had already completed around twenty-five miles of his journey. With the sun sinking in the west, he rode along the bottom of a valley. About two miles ahead, he could see the start of the woodland which fringed that section of the Saline River he must cross to take the most direct line to Vaden.

A bullet, coming from the rear and to the right, made its eerie "splat!" sound as it split the air a few inches from

---

† Texans do not use the word "cinch."

Dusty's head. Although startled by the unexpected—and never pleasant—noise, he did not panic. Like all Texans, he held his reins so that their split ends dangled downwards over his palm, gripped between his thumb and forefinger.* Slackening his grip so that he did not make a sudden jerk at the black's mouth, he stood in his stirrups and twisted his torso in the direction from which the missile had come. What he saw caused him to growl a curse, turn to the front, sink back to the saddle and prepare to increase speed.

Some twenty blue-clad riders had topped the incline. One of them had a Springfield carbine at his shoulder, smoke curling from its .58-calibre muzzle. Going by the way the lieutenant and sergeant of the Yankee party turned on him, the soldier had opened fire without orders. Certainly he had not done his companions any favour, for his actions had deprived them of the best chance they would be likely to get of taking the Confederate officer by surprise.

"I'll bust your guts when we get back——!" threatened the sergeant.

"You stupid son-of-a-bitch!" screeched the officer, then swung from the man to see their proposed victim's horse increase its speed. "Get after him, men!"

Letting out excited yells, sounding almost like a pack of hounds receiving their first sight of the prey, the Yankees started their horses running down the incline. Last to move was the man whose shot had set them up for a long chase instead of what they had hoped would be an easy capture.

Settling down on the saddle instead of posting, Dusty loosened his reins and nudged the stallion's ribs gently with his heels. It was a signal that, taken with the slackening of the pressure on the bit, the horse fully understood. Build-

* The Californian or Mexican usually holds his reins beneath his little finger and up to hang forward over the top of his hand.

ing up momentum, its gait changed from the diagonal-striding, two-beat time of the trot. Instead the right hind hoof struck the ground, then the off fore and left hind simultaneously, and lastly the near fore came down to start the sequence again.

From a trot, the stallion began to canter then opened out to a full gallop. Under-foot, the ground was ideal for fast travelling; the grama grass, short, springy, cushioning the impact of the hooves. Crouching forward at the waist, but maintaining perfect balance and control, Dusty kept his mount collected and prevented its inborn tendency to rush onwards at an ever-increasing speed until it was bolting rather than galloping under his command.

No more shots came, but that did not cause Dusty any especial joy. From what he had seen, the Yankees belonged to the New Hampstead Volunteers. Raised and financed by General Buller, as a means of obtaining his rank — and the social benefits that went with it in time of war — the regiment was not the best outfit in the Union's Army of Arkansas.

Under normal conditions, Dusty would have been in little or no danger of capture. On his other missions into the Yankee territory east of the Ouachita or Caddo Rivers, he had his full Company along. With those sixty expert fighting men at his back, he could have routed the outnumbered Volunteers. Even on the outward journey to Pine Bluff, the situation would not have been desperate. He and his two companions were not only travelling with the bare essentials, but each had ridden a three-horse relay.

As his men had greater distances to cover, Dusty had loaned each of them one of his reserve mounts. In that way, Sergeant Kiowa Cotton and Corporal Vern Hassle could attain a higher speed. It had been a sound decision, for the two non-coms had the better chances of finding one or more of the "tin-clads" at their destinations.

So Dusty was left with only his black stallion. Apart from a couple of blankets rolled in a rubberised-cloth, water-proof poncho, strapped to the cantle, his saddle had no other burden. He had left his Henry rifle—a battle-field capture—at the Regiment's headquarters and at that moment his field-glasses were headed towards Arkadelphia with the mount loaned to the corporal. Unfortunately, the stallion was far from fresh after covering so many miles. If the Volunteers should be adequately-mounted and reasonable riders, he would be hard-pressed to escape from them.

Heading towards the woodland, Dusty could feel the big horse straining under the exertion. To his rear, the Volunteers showed no sign of opening out the hundred or so yards which separated them from him. Nor could they decrease the distance; although it might have been a different story if Dusty had been heavier, or a less skilled rider. As it was, he maintained his lead. Yet he knew that the Yankees would run him down if they stuck to his trail for long enough. Dusty grew more certain of that with each sequence of the black's galloping gait.

There was one way out; although Dusty—a Texan—hardly cared to consider it. Yet consider it he must. Unless something happened to halt the Volunteers, a remote contingency under the circumstances, he knew that he would have to put his scheme into operation should an opportunity to do so arise. They would surely catch up with him if he stayed afork the lathered, flagging stallion for he might easily run it into the ground. So he intended, if the chance presented itself, to quit the black's back, take cover, and allow his pursuers to continue chasing the unencumbered animal.

A desperate risk, maybe, but well worth trying. Without his weight on its saddle, the big horse stood a chance of

outdistancing the burdened mounts of the Volunteers. In
the thick tangle of the woodland, they would be following
their prey by sound, with only an occasional, flickering
glimpse of it caught through the trees. Given just a smidgin
of good Texas luck, the Yankees might go for a mile or
more before they became aware of his deception.

Unless the Volunteers caught it, the range-bred stallion
would eventually return to the Texas Light Cavalry's camp
at Prescott, which it now regarded as its home. If the horse
should be captured, or fail to return for some other reason,
Dusty would have to count its loss, along with that of one
of his saddles, as the price he had paid for retaining his
freedom. For his part, he would only be left afoot until he
had walked the five miles beyond the Saline River to the
home of a Confederate sympathiser who kept a few horses
and saddles hidden away for just such emergencies.

So, much as he hated the whole notion, Dusty started to
make his preparations for carrying it out.

Never forgetting to maintain his balance and keeping the
same steady, controlling pressure on his mount's mouth,
Dusty knotted his reins around the saddlehorn. When he
released them, he wanted the reins to hang loosely against
the stallion's neck instead of trailing free. Like the majority
of range-horses, the black had been trained to come to a
halt and remain reasonably still when the split-ended reins
dangled loose close to its fore legs.

The woods lay close ahead. Although the sun's lower
side was almost touching the western horizon, Dusty knew
that the darkness would not descend quickly enough to
save him. So it had to be the scheme after all. Turning
carefully on the saddle's seat, he looked back. While the
Volunteers had come no closer, they showed no sign of
quitting. So he could not commence his plan of escape
immediately.

Guiding the stallion with expressive hands, thighs and knees, Dusty steered it between the trees or avoided various clumps of bushes, rocks or other hazards. Ahead was a deep, wide valley with sloping sides down which a skilled man could ride at speed. Beyond it was just the thing Dusty needed in his plan.

Such was the rapport between the stallion and its small, efficient master that it did not hesitate on arriving at the edge of the incline. Over it went, going down in a rapid slide, hind legs tucked under its belly and fore legs reaching out ahead. Thrusting his feet forward, Dusty leaned his body to the rear. Coming near to the bottom, the horse gathered itself and thrust away from the slope to light down on level ground. With hardly a break in its motion, it headed across the valley and started up the other side. Dusty once more assumed his upright posture.

"Come on, men!" screeched an excited voice as Dusty's straining stallion completed the ascension. "If he can do it, so can we!"

Darting a glance across his shoulder, Dusty saw the Volunteers plunging into the valley. All of them went, he noticed gratefully. Then he turned to the front and made ready. Ahead was a big old white oak tree, its heavily-foliaged branches offering sanctuary and a safe hiding-place—if Dusty could reach them.

Another swift check on the rear told Dusty that none of the Volunteers could see him. Carefully he eased back until he could raise his feet to the seat of the saddle. Then he stood up, balancing on the fast-moving stallion with the ease of a circus performer. What had been a trick learned to improve his skill as a horseman—and, like his ambidextrous ability, as a means of taking attention from his small size as a boy—now served a most useful purpose.

They were passing under the outer fringes of the tree's

spread of branches. Ahead, a sturdy limb stretched across in a manner ideally suited to the small Texan's needs. Gauging the distance with his eyes, Dusty thrust his arms above his head.

Would he make it?

The question ripped through Dusty's head and received its answer. Fingers curled, his reaching hands slapped against the top of the branch. An instant later the black had passed from beneath his feet, racing onwards under the inborn impulsion to run when being pursued.

Drawing himself upwards with all the strength in his powerful shoulders and arms, he rested the tops of his thighs against the branch. Then he thrust his feet forward with all the force he could muster and tilted his body to the rear. Under the power of the swing, his legs started to rise into the air. During the brief moment he hung upside down, his campaign hat slipped off. Unable to stop it, Dusty hoped that the Yankees would not draw the correct conclusion on seeing the hat under the tree. Completing a semi-circle, Dusty came to a halt laying belly-down on the limb. Hooking his right leg upwards, he mounted the branch to rise and climb until he had put the thickness of the trunk between himself and the valley.

Peering cautiously around the trunk and through the dense foliage, Dusty felt sure that he was hidden from the Volunteers. In fact he could only obtain a limited view of the valley's rim. Already the blue hats of the Yankees rose into sight. Going by what he could see, Dusty concluded that the Union lieutenant was holding all the party in a bunch. Certainly there were no stragglers as they appeared up the incline.

Without the need for conscious thought, Dusty's right hand crossed to draw the left side Colt from its holster and his thumb eased back the hammer. For a moment he thought that he would need the firearm.

"There he is!" roared an excited New England voice.

"Keep after him, men!" urged the officer an instant later. "We'll get the son-of-a-bitch Reb before dark."

A faint grin twisted at Dusty's lips as he realised the Yankees had either heard or seen the stallion without realising that it no longer carried a rider. From the glances he obtained as they approached the tree, sufficient of them had lost their head-dress during the chase that they attached no importance to the sight of his campaign hat laying on the ground.

Urging their horses to greater efforts, the Yankees passed under Dusty on either side of the tree. None of them looked up and they went crashing away on the wild-goose chase. Letting them get about a hundred yards away, Dusty returned his Colt to leather. Going to the limb on which he had swung from the stallion, he lowered himself and dropped to the ground. Collecting his hat, he donned it with a grin.

"Good ole Dick," Dusty mused as he started to walk in the direction of the Saline River. "I'm surely pleased you had me wear these cavalry boots."

Being a long-serving soldier, although he had always been employed as an officer's servant, Dusty's striker, Dick Cody, disapproved of the small Texan's flouting of the *Manual of Dress Regulations*. So, to please Cody, he had agreed to wear breeches and boots that conformed with what amounted to the striker's bible. At that moment, Dusty felt thankful that he had done so.

Maybe the high heels of Texas range-boots held in the stirrup-irons with extra safety, or could be spiked into the ground when roping afoot, but they were pure hell to wear while walking any distance. The much lower heels on his cavalry-pattern boots would allow him to reach the sympathiser's home without too much discomfort.

Yells from the Yankees brought Dusty to a halt. They had only gone about half a mile, according to the sounds, but already knew they had been tricked. Then he heard the crack of a revolver shot, followed by a scream of pain. That sound did not emerge from human lips. For a moment Dusty stood, cold and angry, wondering if one of the Volunteers, furious at the discovery, had put a bullet into the stallion. Then he decided it was not so. Instead the sound reminded him of the squeal a pig made when it felt the prick of a butcher's knife.

Putting aside the question of why the Yankees would shoot at a pig, assuming one should be in the woods, Dusty walked on. He remained alert, giving his attention mainly to the area in which his enemies had disappeared. The precaution paid off when he saw two of the Volunteers riding in his direction. Darting into the concealment of a near-by clump of buffalo-berry bushes, Dusty crouched with the right side holster's Colt cocked in his left hand. Going by their lack of response, the Yankees had failed to notice him walking along, or during his dive into hiding.

Carefully parting a couple of branches with his right hand, Dusty decided that it would have been surprising if the Yankees *had* seen him. They rode side by side at a walk, making only the slightest pretence of searching the surrounding woods for the Rebel officer who had eluded them. Instead they talked to each other and, as they drew nearer, Dusty found their conversation enlightening.

"'Spread out, go back and look for him,' the stupid son-of-a-bitch tells us," growled the taller of the pair, a surly-faced hard-case who slouched like a sack of potatoes on his jaded, sweat-lathered horse. "'Find him,' he says.

'The peckerwood* bastard can't have gotten far.'"

"He can't have, Fred," the other Volunteer pointed out, almost apologetically.

"Can't hell, Simmy!" spat the big man. "He could've dropped off his hoss any time 'tween that valley and where we first saw he wasn't on its back."

"I thought we'd got him when the lufft threw that shot into the bushes," Simmy declared, grinning broadly at the memory. "Lord! His face when that damned great critter bust out. What was it, Fred, a grizzly bear?"

"Just you pair keep coming the way you are," Dusty breathed, studying the incautious approach. "You do that, and I'll be riding again afore nightfall."

If the two Volunteers continued on their present course and without paying a greater attention to duty, they might easily supply him with horses. Bursting out of the bushes, he could throw down on them and either shoot, or make them dismount and surrender their horses. In "Fred's" case, it would probably have to be the former. There was a truculence about him that might be accompanied by a reckless imprudent nature. To achieve his intentions, Dusty wanted the men much closer before he made his appearance.

"Naw!" Fred answered. "It was a hawg of some kind!"

"I never saw a hawg that size," Simmy protested. "Why it was as——"

The ringing notes of a bugle cut off the words. With a feeling of annoyance, Dusty recognised the sound of the "Recall." Reining their horses to a stop at a distance which precluded the chance of him taking them by surprise, the soldiers looked towards the source of the martial music.

* Peckerwood: derogatory name for a white Southerner.
† Luff: uncomplimentary term for a 1st lieutenant.

Dusty remained hidden. To make an appearance now would only stir up gun-play. While he knew that he could shoot accurately enough to tumble both men from their saddles, the horses would bolt before he could stop them.

"Come on," Fred growled. "Looks like he's finally got good enough sense to call it off."

"I ain't sorry about that," Simmy replied. "Now maybe we'll get back to camp in time for supper."

Watching the soldiers ride away, Dusty let out an exasperated grunt. No Texan from the range country cared for walking. However, seeing that it could not be helped, he waited until the sound of the Volunteers' departure had faded into the distance and then resumed his journey.

Satisfied that his pursuers had given up the chase, Dusty kept alert for another possible—and probably greater—danger. According to the conversation he had overheard, the Volunteers' lieutenant had fired at what he believed to be a hidden man and wounded a pig of some kind. That the wound had not been fatal was a factor to be taken into consideration. Dusty had no wish to meet up with the injured animal.

At best the pig would be only semi-domesticated; turned loose by its owner to forage in the woodland, then rounded up in much the same way that Texans raised their cattle. Like longhorns, some of the pigs were never recaptured and reverted to the wild. There were few more dangerous animals in Arkansas than a feral-hog, for it had no inherited fear of human beings. The feral-hog might be cautious and, like an old *ladino* longhorn, try to avoid contact with men; but it would never hesitate to attack if cornered or hurt.

Darkness came without Dusty running into any kind of trouble or danger. He guessed that the ford was not far ahead when he heard the sound of running water. Much to his annoyance, he noticed a small red glow rising among the trees.

"Damn the luck!" Dusty growled, *sotto voce*. "There's somebody bedding down for the night by that blasted ford."

Going by the size of the blaze, it would only be serving the needs of a small party. Nor could Dusty see other glows to tell him that more than one group of men were settling in ahead.

Which raised a couple of vitally important points.

How many men would he be dealing with and would they be friends of foes?

Going by the lack of effort taken to conceal the flames, he would be willing to bet on the maker of the fire being a Yankee; most likely one of a small band. Soldiers, maybe. Or even worse, guerillas, those human wolves who used "patriotism" as an excuse to raid, loot, pillage or murder. Rumour had it that an especially ruthless bunch of Yankee irregulars had moved into this section of the Saline River country. Being captured by them was not a situation any Southerner wished to face. Of course, the fire might have been made by a single soldier riding dispatch.

Not that Dusty felt inclined to go and investigate right then. Common sense dictated that he should put off the attempt until morning. Stalking an unknown area, with an unspecified number of men in it, was not a business he wished to try in the darkness of the night. Far better to make camp in what comfort he could manage until daybreak and then—when able to see where he was putting his feet—move in. Once he had examined the clearing in which the man—or men—rested, he could make an estimation of his best line of action.

With that in mind, Dusty gave thought to his own bed for the night. Up so close to a possible enemy, he could not light a fire. Nor dare he chance breaking branches to make a lean-to. That left him only one alternative, to use the ground for a mattress and the sky as blankets.

"Way my luck's going," Dusty told himself, "it'll pour with rain all night." Then he grinned, thinking of his ever-pessimistic sergeant major, and continued, "Damned if I'm not catching the Billy Jack's."

Having delivered that sentiment, he found a small hollow in a clump of bushes. Packing his hat with leaves, he set it down to be used as a pillow. Taking off his gunbelt, he removed the left-side Colt. Preferring to be cold than left without serviceable weapons, he removed his tunic and rolled the gunbelt in it. Then, with the Colt in his right hand shielded as well as possible by his body, he lay on his right side and went to sleep.

Despite the loosely packed soil among the bushes offering anything but a soft, comfortable bed, Dusty contrived to sleep all through the night. With the dawn's first pink glow creeping into the eastern sky, he woke and sat up. Grunting a little, he came swiftly but cautiously to his feet. The chilly sensation rapidly left him. For all his gloomy, Billy Jack-esque predictions the previous evening, the weather had remained both warm and fine. Having spent many nights bedded down in the open air, although invariably with the protection of blankets and a waterproof poncho, he felt little the worse for his experience.

As Dusty worked the slight stiffness from his limbs, he shook away the light sprinkling of dew that had settled on him. His eyes turned in the direction of the ford. Clearly whoever had camped there also believed in early rising. Already the fire was sending up a column of smoke that told of a recent refuelling. If Dusty intended to move in, reconnoitre and, given the chance, obtain a mount for himself, he must waste no time.

Drawing a bandana handkerchief from his breeches left hip pocket, he carefully wiped all traces of dew from the Colt in his right hand. Fortunately Colonel Sam Colt's workmen had produced a piece of machinery that stood up very well to mild wettings. Dusty knew that the percussion caps prevented moisture from seeping into the cylinder's chambers through the holes in the cap-nipples. The larger openings at the other end of the cylinder were coated with grease, to hold the bullet firmly in position and to stop the flames from the uppermost charge reaching and setting off the other five's loads.

With that basic precaution taken, Dusty thrust the Colt temporarily into his waist-band. Unrolling the tunic, he produced the gunbelt. No damp had reached the second revolver, he noticed with pleasure. Returning the gun from his waistband to its holster, he laid the belt across his hat and put on his tunic. After buttoning the double-breasted front, he strapped on the belt and tied down the tips of the holsters. Emptying the leaves from his hat, he returned the crushed crown to its normal shape and placed it on his head. Dressed and armed, he eased himself through the bushes and started walking with great caution towards the rising column of smoke.

Making use of every bit of the skill and experience he had gained while hunting alert, elusive whitetail deer back home in the Rio Hondo country, Dusty passed through the woodland without a single unnecessary noise. Although many of Buller's command were city-born, he had some country-dwellers. Most of Verncombe's 6th "New Jersey" Dragoons—despite their title—had seen service in Indian campaigns before the War. So it was possible that whoever was camping near the ford possessed keen ears and a knowledge of the danger presented by that kind of terrain. Dusty intended to take as few chances as he could manage.

Watching where he put his feet, so as to avoid stepping on and breaking dry twigs, he also made certain that his clothes did not brush against the trunks of trees or bushes' branches. In the latter he was helped by the figure-hugging nature of his uniform and decided to comment to his striker upon one advantage of the skirtless, non-*Regulations,* tunic; the fact that it had nothing to flap about as he made a stalk through wooded country.

Feeling the wind blowing into his face, coming from the direction in which he was headed, Dusty felt a further sense of relief. Maybe the man, or men, about the fire would be city-dwellers, but their horses would be on the alert. So he knew that having his scent blown away from them would lessen the chances of their detecting his presence and giving a warning.

At last he came into sight of the clearing. Inching forward with even greater care, he halted behind the thick trunk of a burly white ash tree. From the concealment of the five foot wide trunk, he studied the clearing by the ford—and found himself faced with a problem. Although there were two horses hobbled and grazing on the edge of the river's bank, he could see only one man in the open space before him.

Was the man alone, riding a relay, or did he have a companion who had gone off into the bushes for some reason?

Calmly Dusty examined the mystery and drew his conclusions. The two horses were fine animals, a dun and a chestnut, both geldings. They had a powerful, yet not clumsy muscular development that hinted at *brio escondido,* hidden vigour, or stamina and guts well above average. Each had a set of hobbles attached to its forelegs above the pastern joints. U.S. cavalry hobbles, from the look of them, made of two buckle-on leather cuffs connected by a short swivel-link chain.

A pair of officer's pattern McClellan saddles lay on their sides by the fire. Across the seat of one hung a fringed buckskin shirt on which rested a pair of ivory-handled, octagonal-barrelled Colt 1851 Navy revolvers. A tight-rolled multi-hued silk bandana, a black sash of the same material and a low-crowned, wide brimmed grey Stetson hat were draped on the saddle's hornless pommel. Leaning against the seat of the second saddle was a Henry rifle in a fancy-decorated, fringed Indian medicine boot. Dusty could see only one bedroll alongside the fire.

"Not but the one cup there, too," the small Texan mused, staring longingly at the small coffeepot which steamed and bubbled merrily near the flames. "That *hombre's* sure acting obliging."

Naked to the waist, showing a heavy-shouldered, lean-waisted, muscular back, the man in question would be one or two inches over the six foot mark. While he wore U.S. cavalry breeches, his lower legs were encased in knee-high Indian moccasins. The hilt of a long-bladed fighting knife showed above the top of the right moccasin and he kept up his breeches with a fancy-patterned Indian belt. Shoulder-long tawny hair added to Dusty's suspicions that the man was a civilian scout rather than a serving member of the Union Army.

The small Texan knew that several such specialists had been brought from their duties with the Western garrisons and allocated to various Union commands in the hope of combating the South's very effective cavalry raiders. The man was the first of them Dusty had seen in Arkansas.

What the man's features might be like, Dusty could not

tell. Standing with his back to the young captain, the scout
was shaving with the aid of a small steel mirror fixed to the
trunk of a tree. Fortunately his position would prevent him
seeing Dusty reflected on the shining surface.

Even as Dusty prepared to step out from behind the
white ash, he heard the dun gelding let out an explosive,
warning snort. Freezing in his tracks, right hand filled with
the butt of its Colt, he glanced at the animals and saw the
chestnut toss its finely shaped head in alarm.

At first Dusty thought that the horses had located him in
some way. Then he realised that their attention was focused
on the other side of the clearing. Turning his gaze that way,
he saw something big, black-looking and vaguely menacing looming through the bushes. Then the long-haired
scout drew Dusty's eyes his way.

Throwing a quick look at his horses, the man snapped
his head around to face the cause of their agitation. Dusty
formed an impression of tanned, good-looking features
with a neatly trimmed moustache making an almost white
slash above a half-shaven chin.

Clearly a man long used to making rapid decisions, the
scout flung one quick glance towards the bushes then made
as if to spin around and leap to his armament. At which
point, his luck ran out. In turning, his right foot struck the
top of one of the tree's roots. Slipping from the moss-
encrusted surface, it threw him off balance. Discarding his
razor as he went down, he fell into deadly danger.

Snuffling, grunting and grinding its tusks against each
other with a spine-chilling, blood-curdling sound, an enormous pig lunged into the clearing. What had appeared to
be black skin proved to have the deep reddish tint that
hinted of Duroc breeding. However, the hog showed none
of the Duroc's normally docile nature nor much of its
broad-backed, thick bodied build. Tall, standing much

higher at the shoulders than the hips, body fined down until it looked all sinew and hard muscles, it had a long nose and a big, powerful-jawed mouth from which showed tusks almost six inches in length. A raw-looking, bloody furrow on its rump explained its bad temper. Maybe its grandparents had been pure, or part, Duroc, but that hog was closer to a wild boar in its appearance than it was to a domesticated pig.

At the sight of the bristling, squealing horror charging towards their master, the two horses let out startled squeals. They backed away as fast as their hobbles would allow them, not yet in a panic, but close to it. Dusty wanted one, or both, of the geldings—although, to give him credit, he would have intervened even if he had not. So he sprang from the bushes, ready to save the scout from a terrible mauling if he could.

Coming to a halt on spread-apart, slightly bent legs, he inclined his torso to the rear. Doing so rested his weight on the pelvic region and utilised the body's bone structure as added support. At the same time, he swung the Colt forward and up. His left hand rose to cup under the bottom of its mate. Holding the revolver at arms length and shoulder-high, he set the low-blade, white brass tip of the foresight in the centre of the V-shaped notch cut as a rearsight in the hammer's lip.

There was only one hope of stopping the hog in time and doing it called for a very careful aim. Aligning the sights, Dusty squeezed the trigger. The gas from thirty grains of black powder detonating spun a 219-grain conical bullet through the rifling grooves of the seven-and-a-half inch long "Civilian" pattern barrel.* Propelled through the air, the lead made a sharp crack as it ploughed through the

---

* The standard, Army barrel was eight inches in length.

hard bones of the hog's skull. Hitting right where Dusty had intended it should, a couple of inches above the eyes and in the exact centre of the head, the .44 bullet tore into the beast's brain pan. Killed instantly, the hog's forelegs buckled under it and the great body turned a forward somersault from its momentum.

Twisting himself over in a violent, desperate roll, the scout barely avoided being struck by the hog's fast-moving carcass. It crashed to the ground on its back and, with a final, frantic thrashing of its legs, went limp. Raising himself on to his hands, the scout looked at the dead hog. Then he turned his face towards his rescuer. Surprise flickered across the scout's bronzed features as he realised that he owed his life to a Confederate States' Army captain.

"Thanks, frie——" the scout had begun to say, but the words trailed off and, after staring for a few seconds, he continued, "Well I'll be damned!"

"Maybe you'll have time to repent from your sinful ways, *hombre*," Dusty answered, having deftly cocked his Colt on its recoil and turned it to line with disconcerting inflexibility in the man's direction. "Happen you stay put for a spell, that is."

Drawing one leg up under him ready to make a dive towards his weapons, the scout remained at the foot of the tree. His eyes flickered to the hole in the hog's skull, then swung to estimate the distance from which the *big* Texan had cut loose. That had either been a real lucky, or mighty well-aimed shot. Noticing the other's quietly competent appearance, the scout went for the latter choice.

"Was you wanting me dead," the scout remarked, raking Dusty from head to foot with his eyes, "you'd've let the hawg get me."

"Don't you going setting too much store by *that*, *hombre*," the small Texan warned. "If I'd let it happen, the noise'd likely've spooked off your horses and I need them."

"And I thought it was me you liked," said the scout, right hand moving slowly towards his leg.

"While you're down there, take out the knife and toss it this way," Dusty ordered. "With the tips of your fingers, so there'll be no temptation to let you get 'damned' permanent."

Grinning resignedly, the scout obeyed. Drawing the knife between the extreme tips of his thumb and forefinger, he spun it across the clearing and made certain that it never looked like reaching his rescuer. That Texan captain might be young, but he packed a whole heap too much savvy to play games against. Going by the manner in which he handled the Colt, he rated high in skill at using it. No man could take chances with that level of talent to his own advantage. Trying to jump him, without the help of a suitable distraction, would be rapidly fatal. So the scout intended to comply with the other's orders—unless a real good chance of altering their status happened to come up.

"Ole 'Californy' Bill allus told me washing and shaving regular's plumb dangerous," commented the scout. "Damned if he didn't have him a mishap and tell the truth for once."

"It happens to most of us, one time or another," Dusty replied. "You can get up's long's you do it slow and easy."

"Thanks," answered the scout and came to his feet in a lithe, effortless manner that told Dusty he was neither slow nor clumsy in his movements. "Why'd the hawg jump me?"

"Going by that nick on its butt-end, I'd say it was riled 'cause a Yankee luff threw a bullet at it yesterday."

"Why'd he do a fool thing like that?"

"Heard it moving in some bushes, figured it was me and

come up smoking. I'd say he was lucky that ole hawg went away instead of coming at him."

"You see it happen?" asked the scout.

"Heard a couple of Volunteers talking about it while they was supposed to be hunting for me."

"Buller's bunch, huh? That figures. There's not one of them from the Bully his-self down to the lowest drummer-boy's's got sense enough to pound sand into a rat-hole. What you got in mind to do with me?"

"Now I'd say that depends on you," Dusty answered. "I won't chance leaving you hawg-tied here, or having you free to come after me."

"Maybe you should've let the hawg get me," commented the scout.

"There's some's'd say you're right," Dusty admitted. "Trouble being I didn't and it's too late now. After I've got your guns, you can come over and get dressed."

"Can I finish my shave first?"

"Go to it. Only don't try shaving *me* while you're at it."

Keeping a watch while the scout went ahead with his interrupted ablutions, Dusty lowered his Colt and crossed to the fire. Asking for and receiving permission he poured out a cup of coffee. At no time did he relax his vigilance, as the scout observed through the mirror. Dusty presented his captive with no opportunity to jump him, or to make a dash for cover. Finishing the coffee, he collected the Navy Colts and thrust them into his waistband. Then he returned his revolver to its holster and, selecting a moment when the scout had the razor to his tight-stretched throat, slid the Henry rifle from its boot. Working the lever, Dusty emptied the repeater's chamber. While replacing the Henry in the medicine boot, Dusty produced his Colt again.

"Now what?" inquired the scout, having finished his

shave and rinsed his face at the river's edge.

"Come and get dressed," Dusty answered. "Then you can saddle both horses."

"Both?"

"Sure. I'll use one and you'll come with me. Then when I'm safe with my own folks, you can come back with both of them."

"That's sure white of you," commented the scout, certain that the other would keep his word.

"More smart than white," Dusty corrected with a grin. "It's that way, or leave you dead. I don't want a Yankee Injun scout coming hunting for me because I took his favourite horses and guns."

Also grinning, the scout rolled his razor, shaving brush and soap into a canvas hold-all. When he walked towards the fire, he noticed that his captor backed away to a safe distance. Although the Army Colt dangled with its muzzle directed at the ground, the scout figured it could be swiftly brought into line if he made a wrong move. Clearly the moment to reverse their positions had not yet arrived.

Picking up his shirt, the scout drew it on. He discovered, on his head emerging through the neck-hole, that the Texan had taken advantage of his actions to go and collect the horn-handled, clip-pointed fighting knife. For a moment the scout felt uneasy, knowing that the Sheffield, England, firm of W. & H. Whitehead had engraved the message "DEATH TO TRAITORS" along the eight-inch blade, to appeal to purchasers of Unionist persuasions.

"Nice sentiment," drawled Dusty and tossed the knife to the scout's feet. "Put it back in its sheath and leave it there."

Obeying, the scout next knotted the bandana about his throat. He tilted the Stetson into place on his head and

gathered up the sash. For the first time, Dusty realised that
the sash was made of two sections of the silk, one stitched
on top of the other. No, not stitched all the way round. On
either side, above the hips when the sash was in place, the
sections were not connected.

"How do you find it is to draw from that sash, friend?"
Dusty inquired, guessing at the purpose of the unstitched
areas.

"Easy—and fast," answered the scout. "Once you get
the hang of it."

"I'd sooner have holsters myself," Dusty commented.

"Every man to his own taste, Cap'n," the scout said. "I
find I can fetch 'em out a whole heap faster this way."

"Like you say," Dusty drawled. "Every man to his own
taste. Now you're dressed, you can saddle up the horses
and we'll pull out."

"You're giving the orders," answered the scout.

Still keeping his distance, Dusty allowed the man to
fold and pack the bedroll. Then he watched while the
other took the necessary items for saddling-up to the waiting horses. Selecting the dun to start work on, the scout
laid the carefully folded blanket on its back. With a prac-
tised swing, he elevated the McClellan saddle into position.

"Tighten the girth and breast collar real good, friend,"
Dusty commanded. "I won't be getting on until I'm sure
you have."

"With a sneaky, suspicious nature like you've got,"
grinned the scout as he obeyed, "you'd make a mighty
good lawman, Cap'n."

Without knowing it, the long-haired Yankee had just
made a mighty prophetic statement. In the years following
the end of the War, Dusty would serve with distinction as

marshal in three tough, wild, wide-open towns and leave them tamer, better places at the end of his terms of office.*

"A half-smart lil Texas boy like me has to be sneaky and suspicious," Dusty replied, moving closer to make sure the work was completed to his satisfaction. "Happen he wants to stay alive this side of the Ouach——"

Even as he spoke, Dusty happened to glance across the Saline River. A tall man dressed in a hybrid mixture of Union Army and civilian clothes sat a horse among the trees on the other bank. Big, surly-featured, he had a revolver hanging low on his right thigh. The Burnside hat and the blue tunic he wore bore no insignia. Hanging open, the latter exposed a dirty white shirt.

Becoming aware of the small Texan's preoccupation, the scout figured his chance had come. Silently, he stepped away from the dun. His moccasins made no sound as he took two long strides towards the unsuspecting Rebel.

Finding himself observed, the man at the other side of the river swung his horse around and trotted it back out of sight. Just a moment too late, Dusty realised the chance he had presented to his prisoner. Turning his head, he saw the scout springing towards him. Dusty had not looked away from the other for long, but it had proved to be long enough.

Hurling himself forward with the speed of a cougar plunging from a branch at a whitetail deer, the scout knotted and drove his right fist ahead of him. Rock-hard knuckles impacted against the side of Dusty's jaw. For a moment, as he went crashing to the ground, everything seemed to burst before Dusty's eyes into flashing, brilliant

* Told in *Quiet Town*, *The Trouble Busters*, *The Making of a Lawman*, *The Small Texan* and *The Town Tamers*.

lights. Darkness welled in on him an instant before he sprawled face down on the springy grama grass of the clearing. He did not feel the scout turn him over and unbuckle his gunbelt.

At first Dusty's eyelids refused to function when he tried to open them. Under him, the earth felt hard, the grass rough and his neck seemed to be twisted badly. A throbbing pain beat through his head, stemming from his jaw. Slowly his eyes trembled open, blinking at the sudden influx of light. Then the spinning in his skull started to ebb away. Strength oozed back, along with coherent thought. Slowly he moved his neck, turning his aching head until he could see a pair of calf-long Indian moccasins. Then the light hurt Dusty's eyes and he rolled onto his stomach.

The scout stood several feet away, Navy Colts thrust butts forward in his silk sash. Lounging on spread apart feet, the long-haired Yankee had his hands thumb-hooked into the sash and Dusty's gunbelt dangling over his broad left shoulder. Hearing the Texan stirring, the man glanced his way. Then he returned his gaze to the ford. A splashing sound reached the recumbent youngster's ears. Starting to ease himself onto hands and knees, he looked at the four men who were riding through the water in his direction. They were not a comforting sight to a man in Dusty's present situation.

"Don't try anything, Cap'n," said the scout, speaking from the corner of his mouth and with the minimum of lip movement. "That feller you saw's coming back with his kinfolk."

Two of the riders might easily have been related to the man who had brought Dusty into serious difficulties. All had untrimmed black hair, unshaven, sullen, almost brutish faces with a strong family resemblance and were dressed in a similar manner. None were small and they went down in one-inch steps, the first of them being of the middle height.

Swinging his gaze to the fourth member of the party, Dusty felt an uneasy sense of recognition. From his round-topped, wide-brimmed hat, through his frock coat, string tie, trousers and boots, he wore all black. His grubby shirt might have once been white, but now looked a dirty shade of grey. Gaunt of build, with a bearded, hollow-cheeked face, he had an expression of piety that failed to reach, or match, the savage glow in his sunken, dark eyes. Nor did it go well with the ivory-handled Navy Colt carried in an open-topped cross-draw holster high on his left side. Maybe he would have passed for a circuit-riding preacher of the more severe kind to some people, but Dusty felt certain that he was nothing so innocuous.

All of the men darted glances about them, studying the clearing and its occupants with interest. To Dusty, it seemed that the four were adding up the value of everything before them; horses, saddles, firearms, even himself. He noticed the gaunt man staring at something near where he knelt. Following the direction of the other's gaze, Dusty looked at his Jefferson Davis campaign hat. Sent flying from his head by the force of the blow, or through his collision with the ground, the hat lay with its star-in-the-circle insignia facing the ford.

"Greetings, brother," the gaunt man intoned, swinging from his saddle and allowing his reins to dangle free.

"Howdy," replied the scout, watching the other three dismount, leave their horses ground-hitched and follow their leader on foot towards him.

"Brother Aaron here saw you in dire trouble and need,

brother," the gaunt man continued, indicating the middle-sized of the trio. "And, like the Good Samaritan, we've come to give you succour."

"Now that's right neighbourly of you," the scout answered, "whatever that there 'sucker' might be. Only I'm not needing any, thanks."

"Brother Aaron told us that this transgressor had you prisoner," the spokesman for the quartet declared as they came to a halt. "It was our duty as God-fearful men to come to your rescue."

"Why I'm tolerable obliged to you, reverend," the scout exclaimed in respect-filled tones. "And I sure hope you're around happen I ever come to need rescuing."

"I tell you the peckerwood had him took prisoner, Parson!" Aaron snarled.

"Looks that way," said the scout, "don't it?"

Fooled by the long-haired scout's appearance of youth and confident that the odds were all in his favour, Aaron pushed by the gaunt man. Scowling belligerently, in a manner which had caused more than one victim to show alarm and fright, the man continued with his accusations and stepped closer to the scout.

"That Reb bastard had your guns and was making you do what he wanted. Which's why I fetched the Par——"

"Meaning I'm a liar?" asked the scout mildly.

"You might say that!" agreed Aaron, right hand moving suggestively in the direction of his holstered Remington Army revolver.

Instantly all the mildness left the scout and he once again demonstrated that he could move with considerable speed despite his size. Gliding forward a long step, he swung his left hand almost faster than the eye could follow. With a crack like the pop of a freight-driver's whip, the hard palm of his hand caught Aaron at the side of the head.

Having received a blow from the scout, Dusty could almost feel sympathy for Aaron. Coming as a surprise, and with considerable force, the attack spun the hard-case around in a circle to blunder into the smallest of his companions as the others started to move forward.

Spitting out a vicious curse, the biggest of the party grabbed for his Starr Navy revolver. Going by his response to the threat, the scout had been in other such situations. He responded with the same alacrity which had characterised all of his movements since taking advantage of Dusty's distraction. Although his left hand had been put to excellent use, the right had remained by his side. Turning palm out the fingers wrapped about the hand-fitting white curves of the off-side Colt's butt, while the thumb curled over the hammer spur. Twisting the gun from its silk retainer, the scout turned its seven-and-a-half inch barrel to the left, then outwards. Doing so caused the weapon's thirty-eight ounce weight to cock back with hammer without any effort on the scout's part. From waist level, the .36 muzzle lined itself with unerring precision at the hardcase's favourite navel.

From first to very rapidly-following last, the whole move had been made with smooth, lightning fast, precision. Bringing his down-dropping hand to a quivering halt, a good three inches from the butt of the Starr, the burly hard-case stared as if fascinated at the octagonal-barrelled revolver pointing so unerringly at him.

Dull red crept onto "Parson's" gaunt face and his eyes glowed with cold, savage rage; but he stopped his hand in its cross-the-body motion, well clear of his revolver. On separating, the remainder of the new arrivals glowered hate. The only movement made by their hands was the middle-sized man's involuntary raising of his fingers to gently massage his stinging cheek.

Even Dusty, no slouch in matters *pistolero* himself, could not fault the speed and general competence with which the scout had extracted the Colt. Like the other had said earlier, drawing from the folds of a silk sash was fast —providing one took the trouble to learn. Nor was his talent confined to the right hand.

Ejecting the blood that had collected in his mouth, Aaron removed his fingers from the cheek, intending to transfer them to the butt of his gun. Back curved the scout's left hand. It slipped free and cocked the near hip's Colt with almost an equal facility to that displayed when producing the gun's mate. Again the production of a revolver, in a remarkably short space of time, brought a potentially threatening gesture to an abrupt and definite halt.

"As the Good Book says," boomed the man called "Parson." "Raise not thy hand against thy brother, lest the might of the Lord shall smite thee and bring thy pride to dust."

"He ain't *my* brother," the scout pointed out, accepting the quotation as being genuinely from the Bible, but keeping both Colts levelled. "Which I don't take easy to getting called a liar."

"Aaron meant no harm by the words, brother," Parson insisted.

"Men've got killed saying 'em," warned the scout coldly, "harmless or not."

"He spoke hastily, perhaps, brother, but with good and righteous cause," the gaunt man stated and waved a hand in Dusty's direction. "These Secessionist scum killed his parents, good God-fearing folks that they were, and I wouldn't soil your ears with the vileness they did to his sweet, unspoiled sister. Yes, brother, just as dead flies cause the ointment of the apothecary to send forth a stinking savour, so does the sight of that hated uniform bring anger to Aaron's poor and ill-tried soul."

With each word, the angular man's voice raised a pitch until he was thundering the speech as if from a pulpit. He hoped that he would hold the scout's attention for long enough to allow his companions to wrest the advantage from the tanned, tawny-haired Westerner. The hope did not reach fulfilment.

"Likely," was all the scout said, without relaxing his vigilance to a noticeable degree. "So how's it affect me?"

"If you just leave us have that short-growed son-of-a-bitch," Aaron put in with a hint of sarcasm. "We'll hand him his needings."

"I'd surely admire to do it, *brother,* for your poor lil sister's sake," the scout declared, sounding as if every word came straight from his heart. "Only I don't reckon ole Colonel Verncombe'd be right pleased was I to show at Little Rock without his prisoner."

Still on his hands and knees, Dusty saw a slight, but definite change come over the quartet. Going by their mutual flashing exchange of glances and general loss of aggressive attitudes, they were aware of Colonel Verncombe's sentiments on the subject of guerillas or other irregular organisations. Senior colonel in the Union's Army of Arkansas, commanding officer of Buller's most efficient regiment, Verncombe was a man whose opinions and desires must be reckoned with by any guerrilla band if it hoped to stay in operation around the Toothpick State.

That the men were guerrillas, Dusty no longer doubted. Their appearance had suggested that such might be the case, as did their behaviour. However, the mention of the name "Parson" had clinched the matter beyond any shadow of a doubt. Falling into the hands of Northern irregulars, especially members of that particular band, was a situation on which no supporter of the Confederate States cared to contemplate. Dusty realised that the scout might very soon have the opportunity to repay him for killing the boar. From what he had said so far, the long-haired Yankee aimed to do just that. In which case, the scout was placing himself in a position of danger. Parson Wightman had the reputation of being a real bad man to cross; and Dusty felt sure that he had guessed the gaunt man's identity correctly.

In the years before the start of the War Between The States, Augustus Wightman had been a hell-fire-and-damnation preacher with his eyes on advancement to a wealthy bishopric. He had selected on the Slavery Issue as offering him the best chance of attaining his ambition. By thundering searing condemnations of all who opposed the abolition of slavery, he had built up a sizeable following in his home city—but the bishopric went to another priest.

From that day on, Wightman had been a changed man. Laying the blame for his failure on slave-owning interests, he had continued his campaign against them. However, what had once been the utterances of a self-seeking, if occasionally devout, man soon developed into the ravings of a religious fanatic of the worst kind.

Soon after the commencement of hostilities, he had enlisted in the Union Army as a chaplain. Eighteen months later, he had been compelled to resign and was unfrocked by his denomination. There had been tales of outrages committed against Confederate prisoners, and uglier stories of Southern women being raped by Negroes at Wightman's instigation. Far too many, in fact, for them all to be lies by the heathen Secessionist trash to discredit a man of the cloth; as he had tried to claim.

Disregarding his protests, the Union Army's top brass had issued orders that Wightman be given the choice of quitting or facing a court-martial. No less quickly, the leaders of his church had removed him from their midst.

Too wise to resist, for he had known just how much truth there had been in the rumors, he had taken the easy way out. Wishing to avoid a scandal, Army and Church had let him go.

By that time, Wightman had gained a taste for power and a delight in the type of activities which had caused his downfall. So he had formed a band of irregulars, gathering together criminal elements and the worst kind of draft-dodgers who evaded service in the Army. It said much for the strength of his personality and acquired dexterity in the use of weapons that he had welded such an evil, motley crowd into a single unit.

Backed by such men, Wightman had commenced a career of murderous atrocity combined with theft. At last, learning that stories of his activities were being published in foreign, pro-Confederate newspapers, the Federal Congress had ordered that Wightman's outfit be disbanded. When he had refused to do so, Brevet-Colonel Frederick W. Benteen, Jnr.,* a man of forcible personality and prompt action, had been assigned to bring Wightman in. Moving swiftly, Benteen's battalion had located and attacked the Parson's band. Although Wightman and some of the leading members had escaped, the rest of the evil crew were killed, captured or sent flying for safety towards the Canadian border.

Left with a mere ten out of over fifty followers, Parson Wightman had drifted from the danger area. His attempts to re-establish himself had been unsuccessful, and he had found no respite in the East. So he had pushed to the west with his dwindling band.

Although rumours had reached the Texas Light Cavalry

*He later served, in his peace-time rank of Major, with General George Armstrong Custer's 7th Cavalry at the ill-fated Battle of the Little Bighorn.

that Wightman's band were in Arkansas and hid-out somewhere along the Saline River, there had been no confirmation. Dusty now found himself in a position to supply proof of their presence—if, of course, he lived long enough and could escape to return and give it.

Standing behind his cocked, lined Colts, the scout kept a careful watch on the quartet. At the same time, he hoped that the small Texan would act in a sensible manner. With luck, the weight of Colonel Verncombe's name would pull them out of their peril; unless the Rebel captain made some move that would trigger off a shooting fracas.

"Be peaceable, brothers," commanded Wightman, darting a coldly-warning glare at Aaron Maxim and his brothers, Abel and Job. "This young man shares with us in serving the blessed cause of defeating the traitorous Secessionists." He looked about him quickly and went on, "Are you alone, brother?"

"Only for a spell," the scout replied.

"Then you are fortunate enough to have companions close at hand?" Wightman insisted.

Interest showed amidst the scowls of the Maxim brothers' faces, but they refrained from making any hostile gestures and awaited the answer to their leader's question. Their future relationship with the scout would depend on what he said.

"'Californy'" Bill's bringing Major Galbraith 'n' Troop "G" along," replied the scout frankly. "They'll likely be about four, five miles back by now."

"How come you ain't with 'em?" demanded Abel Maxim.

"The Major left me to take this Reb captain on to Little Rock while him and the Troop run his Company off," answered the scout, returning the Colts to the slits in his sash. "Should have done it 'n' be headed this way by now. 'Californy' said's how he'd bring 'em on my trail."

From his position to one side, Dusty heard and understood. Unless he missed his guess, the scout was running a desperate bluff to keep them both out of the guerillas' hands. Whoever that long-haired jasper might be, he would make a mighty tough enemy in a poker game. Nothing about him hinted he was telling other than the truth. Replacing the Colts created the impression that, with help so close at hand, he did not need fear the quartet. Even the selection of the distance separating him from "Californy" Bill and Troop "G" of the 6th "New Jersey" Dragoons had been carefully made. The scout did not know from which direction the guerillas had come, or how far behind they had observed. So he had picked a distance to which they would have been unlikely to be able to see; yet close enough for speedy reprisals to be taken in the event of treachery on the part of Wightman's men.

Still weakened by the effects of the scout's blow, Dusty knew that he could not move fast enough to attempt an escape at that moment. So he remained motionless and silent, watching every move and taking in each word. Studying the guerillas' acceptance of the scout's treatment and interplay of questioning glances, Dusty could tell they were uncertain whether the westerner had reinforcements close by or not. So was Dusty, come to that.

Although Aaron Maxim scowled in surly disbelief, he left his doubts unspoken. One taste of the scout's hard hand had been enough for him and he suspected that, if there should be a next time, the response to further criticism might be a bullet. Of the others, only the largest of the brothers raised any comment.

"I didn't know California Bill was hereabouts," Abel growled, looking a mite uneasy and concerned.

"Colonel Benteen lent him 'n' me to the 'New Jersey'

Dragoons for a spell," the scout explained. "Figured us being such all-fired good Injun-fighters 'n' all's we could maybe help 'em ag'in the Texas Light Cavalry. You know ole 'Californy' from someplace, mister?"

"We've heard tell on him," Abel admitted sourly.

"I tell you, I ain't never seen his better at reading sign 'n' following tracks," the scout continued cheerfully, as if imparting information of importance. "Which, I sure didn't try to hide which way we was coming."

If there was one part of California Bill's character upon which the scout did not need to elaborate, it was his ability at following tracks. All of Wightman's party had good reason to remember it.

One of the men who had braved the terrible over-land journey to the West Coast during the gold rush of 1849, California Bill had not made his fortune. Instead, he had received a thorough education in all matters pertaining to Indian warfare. Serving the Union Army as a civilian scout, it had been he—sent East for the duration of the War—who had guided Benteen's battalion to what Wightman's guerillas had fondly believed to be a secret camp.

Frowning, the Parson thought fast. For something over a month, he and his last eight companions—two had deserted on the way west—had been living at a small farm close to the Saline River. They had come to Arkansas in the hope that Buller might take a more lenient attitude than most Union, or Confederate, generals towards their irregular activities. Being wolf-smart, Wightman had advised extreme caution. So they had held off committing their usual depredations, except on a minor scale to obtain the necessities of life, until a sympathiser in Little Rock could discover how the commanding general of the Army of Arkansas would react to their presence in his area.

So far there had been no reply and Wightman knew that his men were getting restless. There were other guerilla bands operating in the Toothpick State, or back East, in which the less well-known members of his outfit might find shelter. So he wanted to be able to give them some definite news as quickly as possible.

Slowly Wightman turned his eyes in the direction of Dusty's hat and he made sure that he had identified its insignia correctly. The Texas Light Cavalry was Ole Devil Hardin's own regiment, organised, financed and equipped at his instigation. For such a small, insignificant youngster to be a captain suggested that he stood high in Hardin's favour. If so, to deliver him into Buller's hands would gain the general's approbation. Perhaps sufficiently so for Buller—hard-pressed and under heavy criticism due to his lack of success against the Rebels in Arkansas—to overlook Wightman's past indiscretions and confer at least a semi-official status upon him.

The only problem being how to obtain possession of the prisoner. Using force did not appeal to the Parson. Not at that moment, anyway. Already the long-haired scout had demonstrated a speed that none of the quartet could equal when drawing their guns. So he would be much too fast for any of them to prevent him from shooting should they force a showdown. Of course their combined numbers would bring them through, but at least one of the four would die. There was an ugly element of chance over which of them it would be that did not appeal to Wightman.

More than that, if the scout had told the truth, killing him would not solve the problem. No matter how they tried, Wightman's inexperienced companions could not hide all signs of the crime from a man like California Bill.

Once the old timer discovered that something had happened to his friend, he would not rest until he had led Troop "G" to the men responsible.

Or was the scout bluffing?

Wightman decided against calling the bluff until he had formed a better impression of what cards the opposition held.

"Then brother," the Parson said, managing to bring a kind of joviality to his sober features. "Why not accompany me to my home and wait for your friends there?"

"Well, I——" the scout began.

"We have heard that there are other Rebels between here and Little Rock," Wightman interrupted. "If you meet them, you might lose your prisoner and your own freedom. I would be doing you a disservice, brother, if I didn't insist you come."

"Wouldn't be right at all," Job Maxim agreed and his brothers rumbled menacing confirmation.

For a moment Dusty thought that the scout intended to refuse. Then he saw the other look across the river and stiffen slightly. There had been a definite challenge in the words. If the scout refused to accompany the quartet, he would have to back his non-compliance with roaring guns. Dusty hoped that he would be able to help in some way. With that in mind, he started to come to his feet.

"You stay put there, you Rebel bastard!" Aaron spat, making as if to advance and clenching his fists.

"Major Galbraith don't take to folks rough-handling his prisoners," the scout stated, moving between Dusty and Maxim.

"He ain't here——!" Abel started to protest.

"Let's just say I'm acting for him," answered the scout evenly. "If you've got nothing better to do, Cap'n, go saddle your hoss."

Shaking his head, for coming into an upright position had started it spinning again, Dusty stood and looked at the scout. He caught a brief, barely discernible nod from the plainsman and decided to obey. Clearly the other did not intend to accept the challenge right then. So Dusty decided that he had better go along with the decision.

Leading the way to the second saddle, the scout picked up the Henry and its fancy medicine boot. Then he stood back and allowed Dusty to collect the saddle. They both noticed Aaron talked animatedly into Wightman's ear and throwing angry glares at them.

"He's sure pot-boiling mad about something," Dusty remarked, gathering the saddle-blanket, bridle and reins in his left hand, while his right held the light McClellan saddle and its breast strap.

"Likely telling the Parson he's certain sure you'd got me prisoner when he come up on us the first time," answered the scout. "Which, if it's believed, 'll make a helluva liar out of me."

Wanting an excuse to prolong the conversation, Dusty allowed his left hand's burden to slip. Although Wightman and the brothers continued to talk in low, argumentative tones, they did not entirely relax their vigilance over Dusty and the Yankee scout.

"So nobody's coming, huh?" Dusty asked, bending to retrieve the equipment.

"Not so's I know on," admitted the scout. "I'd say we're safe until *they* get to know it."

"Why wait?" Dusty inquired. "Just let me grab a hold of one of my guns, accidental-like and we'll shoot our way by 'em."

"I'd thought some of it. Near on done it just now, comes to that."

"What stopped you?"

An increased sense of liking and admiration grew in the scout. At no time had the small Texan looked at the dead pig, or given a single hint to remind him that he owed his life to the other's skill with an Army Colt. Maybe they were serving on the opposite sides in the civil conflict that was tearing their country apart, but the scout figured his captive would do to ride the river with, even if the water should be over the willows. However, the soft-spoken question required an answer.

"There's another son-of-a-bitch of 'em across the river," the scout explained. "And he's got what looks awful like a Spencer rifle pointed slab-dab at us."

At the scout's warning, Dusty turned his eyes to the western bank of the Saline River. He saw the reason for the scout's earlier failure to take up the quartet's challenge. Standing partially concealed by a slippery elm tree, a middle-sized, stocky man looked towards them along the sights of what appeared to be a Spencer repeating rifle. The newcomer's presence threw an entirely different complexion over the affair. If Dusty and the scout tried to escape, his rifle would halt at least one of them.

Carrying the gear towards the chestnut, with the scout by his left side, Dusty saw Aaron Maxim slouching their way. Instead of showing pure suspicion, Aaron's unprepossessing features glinted with triumph. He looked like a man who had finally caught out another in a trick or lie. However, his present feelings of elation did not entirely wipe away his caution, for he halted well beyond the reach of the scout's arms.

"If he was *your* prisoner all along," Aaron challenged, "how come you'd had to knock him down when we rid up?"

"That was your son-of-a-bitching fault," rumbled the scout menacingly. "If you hadn't come slinking and crawling about over the river, I'd not've stopped watching him. He tried to jump me and I had to knock him down."

"Yeah!" snorted Aaron. "Well I——"

"Deacon!" the scout called, not wanting Wightman to guess that his identity had been discovered.

"What is it, brother?" asked the Parson, flashing a triumphant glance to Abel Maxim at the "proof" that the scout did not recognise them.

"I'm getting quick-sick of this jasper riding me," the scout stated flatly. "If he don't quit—and fast—I'll forget how he's suffering over his sister and let windows in his skull. And I'll do it so fast your 'brother' across the river there won't be fixed to stop me."

All the pomp and aggression oozed out of Aaron as the implication of the words struck him. Looking at the threatening figure of the long-haired westerner, crouching lightly on spread-apart, slightly bent legs and with hands turned palms outwards close to the white butts of the Colts, he realised that he might be in imminent danger of being killed. Up to that point, confident that Blocky's presence beyond the ford was unsuspected, Aaron had been all set to face down and call the scout's bluff. Instead of that, the scout was aware of his peril and had spoken the truth to Wightman. Maybe Blocky would down him, but by that time Aaron would probably be too dead to care.

Although learning that the scout had located Blocky handed Wightman a shock, he tried his best to hide it. Despite the gaunt man's objections, Aaron had insisted on going and testing his theory. Wightman had wanted to make sure that the scout did not have friends in the vicinity before taking action, but could not dissuade the hard-case.

Watching Aaron's face, Wightman knew that the other would be only too pleased to be rescued from his predicament.

"Peace, brothers," the Parson intoned as solemnly as if pronouncing a benediction to a wealthy congregation. "Peace, lest one of you, like Nicanor, lays dead in his harness. Curb thy tongue, Brother Aaron, for it is as the crackling of thorns under a pot. And you, stranger, bear with him in his grief, toil and tribulations. To err is human, to forgive, divine."

Only too eager to slip out without loss of face—or life—Aaron grunted what might have been an apology and turned to lurch back to his brothers. Being too wise a man to take the matter further, the scout let the hard-case go without protest or added comment.

"Close," Dusty breathed, continuing his interrupted walk towards the horses.

"*Real* close," agreed the scout. "He looked like to wet his pants when I let on about his 'brother' over there."

For all his apparent calm, the scout felt distinctly uneasy. He knew that the quartet were suspicious, but hoped he had so far avoided confirming their doubts. Possibly the forthcoming saddling of the chestnut would give them further reason to know that he had been lying. Not by the fact that the Rebel captain carried a Union Army McClellan saddle, bearing a metal insignia inscribed with the letters "US" at the intersection of the breast-collar's Y-shape. Shortages of materials in the South had caused its Armies to rely to a great extent on what they could loot from the Yankees.

The chestnut gelding caused the scout's anxiety. Spirited, it required careful and competent handling. Perhaps the small Texan lacked the necessary skill to gain its confidence. If so, the four guerillas would guess that the chestnut did not belong to him. Of course, that could be explained away by a statement that the Rebel had lost his own mount; but the suspicions would increase.

Studying the chestnut as he approached it, Dusty's assessment of its nature coincided with the scout's. Going by the steady manner in which it stood, it was used to being collected by hand rather than roped. So Dusty drew closer at an angle from ahead and towards its near shoulder. Speaking gently and calmly, he laid his right hand on its shoulder. From there, showing no hesitation, he ran his palm across the chestnut's withers, along its neck and to the head.

Watching the manner in which Dusty rapidly gained the gelding's confidence, the scout breathed a sigh of relief. To the quartet hovering in the background, it would seem that the small Texan knew the horse and was treating it in the usual manner.

Satisfied he could deal with the horse, Dusty knotted the separate ends of the reins. He then slipped them over the sleek, well-formed head, but he kept them just behind the ears. Doing so gave him a measure of control over the gelding if it should try to move away from him. With deft ease, Dusty fitted the bridle into position and adjusted the bit in the chestnut's mouth.

Fortunately for himself and the scout, Dusty had handled enough Yankee McClellan saddles to be conversant with their differences from his double-girthed range rig. After placing the folded blanket in position, he draped the right side's stirrup leathers and girth across the seat. Hoisting the saddle into the air, he laid it on the chestnut's back. With the girth tightened and the breast-collar fitted as perfectly as the scout could have desired, Dusty set the stirrups to the level of his shorter legs. He made the latter move under the pretence of testing the fit of the saddle, and avoided permitting the quartet to notice that the stirrup-leathers had been adjusted for a much taller man's use. Freeing the reins from their knot, he held them while he unbuckled the hobbles, which he placed in the left-hand saddle-pouch.

Hanging Dusty's gunbelt across the dun's saddle, the scout secured the medicine boot to the left side of the pommel. Then he removed and put away his hobbles.

"Mount up, Reb," he ordered. "We're all set to go, Deacon."

"Come with us then," Wightman commanded.

"Now I ain't suggesting nothing," the scout said, in a tone that showed he *was*. "But I reckon it'd be safer for 'Brother' Aaron to ride in front of me—Just so's he can stop the Reb here from escaping."

"A goodly notion, brother," affirmed Wightman, silencing Aaron's protests before they could be uttered. "Now I'm a man of peace and know nothing about such things, but shouldn't you fasten that blasphemous Southern dog's reins to your saddle? He may try to seek safety in flight."

"He'll not achieve it with us all 'round him," the scout answered.

"If he does," Abel growled, "we'll stop him for good and all."

"Likely he knows it," said the scout calmly and swung astride the dun. "Come on, I can surely use some breakfast."

Mounting up, the guerillas formed a loose box around Dusty and the scout. Glowering savagely, Aaron went ahead. Wightman rode at the scout's left side and Job moved into position to Dusty's right. Drawing the Mississippi rifle from its boot, Abel brought up the rear. Splashing through the ford, they were joined by the Spencer-toting man on the western bank.

"Who're they, Parson?" Blocky inquired, nursing the repeater across his upper thighs.

"A soldier in the blessed cause, Brother Blocky," Wightman answered. "And a miserable peckerwood wretch who cowardly surrendered himself in the face of the righteous wrath of Colonel Verncombe's Dragoons."

"Verncom——!" Blocky ejaculated, looking around nervously. "Is he——?"

"One of his Troops is coming," Wightman answered. "Until it arrives, I am extending our hospitality to our brother here."

With that, the gaunt man jerked his head to the rear. Allowing the others to ride by, Blocky ranged his mount alongside Abel's and started to converse with him in a low tone. Dusty guessed that Abel was giving Blocky the full story and mentioning Wightman's plans for the future. However, the pair held their voices at such a level that the words did not carry to the small Texan's ears.

Led by Aaron, the party passed through the woods parallel to the river for about half a mile. Then they swung along the banks of a stream that ran through a narrow, woodsided gorge. Turning a corner, Dusty found that the gorge opened out and he received his first sight of the guerillas' camp. An inclination of the scout's head drew Dusty's attention to where, on his right-hand slope, a tall, gangling man sat nursing a Sharps rifle and resting his back against a fallen tree's trunk. Making as if to rise, the man received an imperious downwards wave from Wightman. Guessing at its meaning, he sank back again and resumed his watch on the bend in the gorge.

From the sentry, Dusty turned his gaze to the band's hideout. What he saw filled him with a sense of suspicious contemplation. The small log cabin, with a lean-to at the left and a truck garden to the right, the barn, backhouse and the empty pig-pens down by the stream all looked in too good condition to have been deserted by their owners for any length of time. Dusty wondered what had happened to the people who had lived there.

On arriving at the front of the house, the men spread into a line. Giving the signal to dismount, Wightman swung from his saddle. Then he seemed to be struck by a thought and looked at Abel.

"Will you and Brother Blocky go and see to the horses down in the south forty?" the Parson asked. "I thought that I heard a mountain lion last night and they may be in fear and trembling from the beast."

"Sure, Parson," Abel answered, reversing his direction halfway to the ground. "Come on, Blocky. Let's go see."

"And you, friend," Wightman continued, clearly wanting to prevent the scout from thinking too much about the order. "If you will come with me, we will secure your prisoner in the barn. You will understand, that with Brother Aaron's feelings about the God-less Secessionists, I can neither have him in the house, nor let him partake of our food."

Even with his desire to hang on to Dusty, Wightman could not lessen his bigoted, intolerant hatred towards one of the people whom he blamed for failing to receive the bishopric. That thought more than any other had prompted his words.

"It's your place 'n' your food," the scout answered, although he shared Dusty's thoughts on the absence of the real owners. "Let's go, Reb."

Even as they walked towards the corner of the cabin, the scout realised that he had left Dusty's gunbelt suspended over his saddle. Knowing that to fetch it might arouse suspicion, he made no attempt to do so.

A tall, fairly handsome young man, dressed in the part-military fashion of all the band but Wightman, ambled around the corner towards them. A low-tied holster on his right thigh carried an Army colt, balanced by an empty sheath at his left hip. The knife from the sheath, a long, spear-pointed, double-edged weapon, was in his right hand. Not for any sinister purpose, but to round the one-inch diameter end of a six-inch length of oak branch. From beyond the cabin came the explosive snorts and hoof-stampings of an angry horse, mingled with loud curses.

"What's happening, Charley?" asked Wightman.

"Ole Stap brung in a real fine-looking black hoss," the young man answered. "Trouble being, they ain't getting on too good."

"Let's take a look," Wightman suggested.

On turning the corner, Dusty received a shock. Behind the cabin, concealed from their view by it and the barn, was a small pole corral. At its open entrance, a big, burly young man—apparently a younger member of the Maxim family, clung to the reins of Dusty's black stallion with his left hand. In his right, he held a leather quirt. Even as the man appeared, Stap lashed savagely at the stallion with the quirt. Squealing in pain, it reared high and its front hooves flailed the air. Stap moved back, trying to drag the horse down on all fours. Snarling obscenities, he drew the quirt over his right shoulder and prepared to use it again. If he heard the angry growl and sound of rapidly approaching feet to his rear, the sounds gave no warning of danger to him. However, something closed on the end of the quirt. Before Stap could resist, the whip was wrenched from his fingers.

Hot rage blasted inside Dusty at the sight. Ignoring the danger doing it presented, he hurled himself from among the other men. He had spent much time in winning the stallion's confidence and training it by far gentler means than were usual in the mid-1860's. In return for his kindness, the horse had given him very good service. Only the previous evening, it had even saved his life by its courage, stamina and speed. So he could not stand back and watch it abused by the the foul-mouthed, brutal-faced guerilla.

Four racing strides carried Dusty within distance of Stap. Out stabbed the small Texan's right hand. Gripping the lash of the quirt, he tore it from the other's grasp and flung it aside. Spitting curses like boiling water erupting from a kettle's spout, Stap released the stallion's reins. Already drawing back, the big horse retreated into the corral. Its tormentor swung around, glaring in almost maniacal rage. Finding himself faced by a small, insignificant-looking Rebel captain, Stap let out another screech.

"I'll kill you!" he howled and hurled a power-packed round-house left towards Dusty's head.

With his fist in flight, Stap became aware of a sudden, amazing, almost scaring change come over his proposed victim. Suddenly, miraculously, the Rebel stopped looking small. He seemed to take on a size and heft to make him larger and more powerful than his brawny assailant. Unfortunately for him, Stap noticed the chance too late to halt his attack.

"What the hell!" Job bellowed as Dusty bounded towards his brother.

"I'll stop hi——!" Aaron began, right hand dropping towards his revolver.

"Let him go!" growled Wightman, face alight with sadistic delight. "Your brother will smite him hip and thigh."

Which seemed a reasonably logical conclusion, comparing the six inches difference in Dusty's and Stap's height and the latter's considerable advantage of weight. Stap had a reputation for being a rough-house brawler, with better than fair skill in a brawl. For all his plans to ingratiate himself with General Buller at the Rebel captain's expense, Wightman could not resist the temptation to watch one of the hated Secessionists receive a brutal beating. Even if the scout had told the truth about being followed by a Troop of Dragoons, the injuries inflicted by Stap could be explained away. There was, however, the matter of how the scout would react to the sight.

"You saw how that Rebel filth attacked Brother Stapley without provocation, stranger?" Wightman challenged, looking at the plainsman.

Before the scout could be forced to take a stand on the issue, Stap launched the attack—and they all received something of a shock.

Ducking under the punch, Dusty let the bigger man's impetus bring him forward. Even as Stap realised that his antagonist had almost unsportingly avoided the attack, he started to have troubles of his own. Bowing his legs to take him beneath the other's fist, Dusty kept his right hand braced against the right hip. Like a flash, the small Texan struck back.

The manner in which Dusty held his hand might have looked strange to western eyes, but any student of Oriental *karate* could have warned Stap of the danger. Instead of closing his hand, Dusty bent his thumb across the open and upturned palm. Driven forward, with a slight twisting of the torso to increase their force, the extended fingers thrust into Stap's solar plexus. To the guerilla, it felt as if he had been jabbed with a blunt spike of wood. Breath burst from his lips and he changed from advance to retreat, folding over. Coming down, the centre of his face met with Dusty's left fist as it rose in an occidental fashion. Dusty proved to be almost as effective when striking in the conventional manner.

Almost, but not quite. He had hoped to strike Stap on

the jaw, which would have rendered the guerilla *hors de combat,* or so near to it as not to matter. Instead, the other's withdrawal caused the fist to miss its mark. Not that Stap felt any gratitude over his good fortune. Ploughing into Stap's already unlovely nose, Dusty's knuckles crushed it. The force of the blow lifted Stap erect. Blood gushed from his nostrils as he spun around twice and crashed back-first into the left side gate-post.

"I saw him, for sure," admitted the scout, grinning maliciously. "Ain't he the mean one?"

Once again the small, insignificant-seeming young Texan had won the scout's respect by proving himself to be a mighty capable and efficient *big* man.

Shaking his head, to try to bring sense back into it, Stap reached for his Colt. In his pain and bewildered condition, he did not make anything like a flashing, well-performed draw. Allowing the gun to clear leather and begin to lift in his direction, Dusty lashed up his right leg. Coming inwards, the toe of his boot caught the back of Stap's palm with a force that numbed the hand. Stap's fingers opened and the gun spun away from him. For all that, he responded with some speed. Thrown from his daze by the agony of the kick, Stap focused his eyes on his assailant. Snarling barely coherent curses, Stap whipped across his left arm in a back-hand slap to Dusty's head. Caught with his foot still descending from the kick, Dusty pitched sideways. Once more the small Texan lost his campaign hat.

"Get him, Stap!" screeched Charley excitedly, throwing the piece of wood down in front of him and waving the knife. "Stomp him good!"

Willing to carry out his companion's advice, Stap thrust himself from the gate post. Although the Texan had not fallen, the slap had knocked him back several feet. He looked to be off balance and easy meat for reprisals. Eager to hand them out, Slap hurled himself after Dusty. Extending his arms, the guerilla's big hands reached ready to take hold of the small Rebel.

By the time Stap had drawn near, Dusty was in full control of himself. Coming to a halt facing the guerilla, Dusty side-stepped at the last moment. Pivoting around as the other blundered on, the small Texan caught him by the shoulder and turned him. Then Dusty demonstrated some of the fighting skill which the spy at Pine Bluff had doubted he possessed. Smashing a right cross punch to Stap's jaw, Dusty sent him backwards and kept him retreating with a battery of rapidly-thrown blows to the head and body.

"The stinking peckerwood son-of-a-bitch!" Aaron spat out, his gun still half drawn and allowed to remain that way because he had believed his brother could easily thrash the diminutive Rebel. "I'll fix——"

"Leave the gun be, Maxim!" Wightman hissed savagely, clamping a hold on Aaron's wrist as the other tried to complete the withdrawal. "Like I've been telling you, we need him alive!"

Twisting his head, Aaron stared briefly, but furiously, at the speaker. Then he swung his eyes away from the cold, savage, gaunt face. Experience had taught the guerilla that his leader was never so dangerous, or determined to receive compliance with his wishes, than when he dropped the pious-sounding word "brother" and began to use surnames. Some people might regard Parson Wightman's pomposity and pseudo-religious cantings as harmlessly amusing, but Aaron knew him to be a cold-blooded killer with no scruples against taking even his own men's lives if they crossed him.

So Aaron allowed the revolver to slip back into its holster and jerked his arm from the gaunt man's grasp. Common sense told Aaron that, even if Wightman did not stop him shooting the Texan, the long-haired scout would do it. There was another, almost equally effective way in which he might help his younger brother.

Driven backwards by Dusty's fists, Stap literally did not know from where the next blow was coming. Instead of trying to anticipate the next point to be attacked and guarding it, his hands fled to the last place on which his assailant's hard fists had impacted. Caught by an almost classic left jab to the jaw, he nearly ran rearwards to escape further punishment. To his horror, he saw that the enormous Texan was following with the clear intention of continuing the punishment.

In his eagerness to catch up with the reeling guerilla, Dusty did not notice that he was passing in front of the other men. Then, from the corner of his eye, he saw Aaron lunging in his direction and felt the man's hands close on his right wrist. Bringing himself to a halt with his weight on the right foot, Dusty did not try to jerk his arm free. Instead he threw his left leg to the rear, pivoting himself around. Twisting closer instead of attempting to draw away, Dusty hurled his left arm rearwards and up. It passed over Aaron's clutching hands, propelling the clutched fist at his face. Once again Dusty reverted to *karate*. Knotting his fist so that the second finger's protruding root made the impact, he crashed it against the *philtrum* collection of nerves immediately under Aaron's nose. Sharp agony stabbed through Aaron's head, numbing his brain. Opening his hands, he stumbled away with them flying to his damaged face.

The respite had given Stap a chance to recover. Changing direction, he leapt from behind the Texan. Throwing his right arm across the back of Dusty's neck, he bent the other for a headlock and planned to drive the left fist into his face. Up flashed Dusty's left arm to Stap's left shoulder

and his right hand closed just as quickly on the upper inside of the guerilla's left thigh. Throwing his right leg in
front of Stap's, before the young hard-case could carry out
his second intention, Dusty ducked his left shoulder in the
direction of the ground.

So suddenly did Dusty respond, that Stap was taken by
surprise and pulled off balance. Forcing the guerilla's head
down with his left arm, Dusty pushed strongly at the
trapped thigh while subsiding. Stap's feet left the ground,
rose into the air and described a beautiful semi-circle.
Coming to earth with a solid thud, he felt himself released
and bounced away from his would-be victim.

Once again Aaron tried to come to his brother's rescue.
Darting forward with his hands still trying to lessen the
pain from his nose, he halted between Dusty's spread-apart
feet and raised his right leg. Although Aaron hoped to
stamp his heel into Dusty's groin, the attempt came to
nothing. Hooking his right foot behind Aaron's left ankle,
Dusty drove the sole of his left boot against the other's near
knee-cap. By jerking forward at the ankle and pressing to
the rear of the knee, Dusty sent the burly guerilla toppling
away to crash on his back in the dirt.

Before Dusty could rise, Stap had writhed around and
plunged on top of him. Kneeling astride the small Texan's
torso, Stap smashed a right which twisted his head sideways. Then the young hard-case closed his hands about
Dusty's throat. Raising Dusty's shoulders from the ground,
Stap tried to crash his head against it. By bracing his neck
muscles, Dusty lessened the impact; but he knew that he
must escape.

Then he remembered seeing the length of branch dis-
carded by Charley and recalled something taught to him by
Tommy Okasi, his uncle's Oriental servant. Even as his
upper torso was raised again, his right hand scrabbled for

and found the stick. Down drove Dusty's head, but again
his braced muscles and Stap's weakened condition saved
him from incapacitation. Gripping the stick at its centre,
Dusty lashed his right arm forward and up. The protruding
butt end of the stick below the heel of his hand crashed on
to the bridge of Stap's nose. Instantly the guerilla's brain
seemed to burst into a searing white-hot fire. Screaming,
he took his hands from Dusty's neck and involuntarily
began to rear upwards.

Feeling the weight leave his body, Dusty braced his feet
and head on the ground. Bowing the rest of his frame upwards, he caught Stap between the thighs and pitched the
guerilla head-first from him.

There was need for haste in escaping from beneath Stap.
Already Aaron was starting to rise and Job was moving in.
Aaron hurled himself through the air without regaining his
feet. Bending his knees as he sank into a lying position,
Dusty caught the man's chest on the soles of his boots.
Again the improvised *yawara* stick proved its worth. De-
vised by Okinawans, forbidden by their rulers to carry
arms, the techniques of *yawara* fighting served the small
Texan equally well. As Aaron's weight pressed down on
him, Dusty propelled the rounded butt-end as he had at
Stap—except that this time he sent the hard hemisphere
into his assailant's temple. Aaron's body went limp. Exert-
ing all his strength, Dusty straightened his legs and flung
the unconscious hard-case from him. Using the same impulsion, Dusty threw himself upright.

A low, savage snarl from his right warned him of
danger. Glancing around, he found that Job was rushing
towards him. Already the man's right fist flung at Dusty's
head. Gasping in breaths of air, Dusty dropped into a
kneeling position that carried him beneath the blow. With
his left leg thrust almost straight to the rear and right knee

bent, he looked like a sprinter preparing to start a race. Using much the same methods as a sprinter leaving the blocks, he thrust himself forward. Shooting out before him, the "point" of the stick—that part emerging ahead of his thumb and forefinger—ploughed agonisingly into Job's groin.

Giving a strangled scream of torment, Job fell with his body draped on Dusty's head. Surging erect, the small Texan toppled the man over him. Clutching at the stricken area, and barely conscious, Job crashed to the ground behind Dusty.

Turning, Dusty confronted Wightman, the scout and Charley. In a defensive crouch, he held the *yawara* stick ready for further use. Hissing furiously, Charley lunged forward. Thrusting out his left foot, the scout tripped the young man. Even as Charley sprawled face down, knife flying from his fingers, the scout drew right-handed and threw down on the small Texan.

"Drop it, Reb!" the plainsman ordered, with a slight jerk of his head in the direction of the cabin. "Do it fast!"

Flickering a look that way, Dusty saw a medium-sized, lean guerilla with a revolver in his right hand running from the building. Even before he obeyed the scout's command, Dusty noticed that the other had swung the Navy Colt in Wightman's direction. Opening his hand, Dusty let the stick which had served him so well drop to his feet. He wondered what the scout intended to do next.

"Tell your man not to shoot, Deacon," the long-haired westerner said, pointing his gun by what seemed an accident straight at Wightman's belly.

"Don't shoot, Brother Herbert! Wightman yelped, knowing that the muzzle was turned his way by design not chance. "Do you help that Secessionist scum, stranger?"

"He's still my prisoner," the scout pointed out, then in-

dicated a somewhat dazed Charley who had reached hands
and knees but not stood up. "And I figured you didn't want
no more of your boys abusing."

Looking around him, to where the three brothers lay
either rolling in agony or still and unconscious, Wightman
felt that the scout had a point. While wild and without
moral scruples, Charley was more dangerous from behind
than in front. If that small—or was he small—Texan could
lay low the three Maxim boys, he would make easy meat
of the hot-headed Charley. Wightman had no wish for his
small band to be further weakened, although that might not
matter if——

"Hey!" the scout exclaimed suddenly. "Look where I'm
pointing my gun. It's sure lucky that feller you've got on
guard didn't shoot me or this ole Navy'd right certain go
off."

An icy feeling rose in Wightman's stomach at the
words. Up to that moment he had been hoping that Gustav,
up on the slope, would see what was happening and shoot
the scout down. Now, with sickening clarity, Wightman
realised that such an action would have also caused his
own death. The scout's negligently-held revolver had its
hammer drawn back at full cock under his thumb, while his
forefinger depressed the trigger. If he had been hit by a
bullet, those grips would have relaxed. Before the barrel
could be deflected far enough, a fast-driven, conical-
shaped piece of lead would have ripped into Wightman's
belly. He had seen too many men die gut-shot to relish the
prospect of it happening to him.

Turning fast, he saw the lanky sentry—never the swift-
est of thinkers—raising the rifle.

"All is well, Brother Gustav!" Wightman yelled, anxiety adding a tinny note to his tones. Relief rolled through

him as he saw the rifle lower and its owner run forward. Turning to the scout, he continued, "What would you have us do now, stranger?"

"Best get the Reb there tied up safe in the barn, like we was going to," answered the plainsman. "I'll tend to it while you and the your 'brothers' see to them three fellers' hurts."

"It would be better—and safer for you—if we came with you," Wightman objected. "He has already shown himself mighty in sin and evil. So we will come and make sure he doesn't try his Devil-inspired tricks on you. Take up your knife, Brother Charley and put it in its sheath."

Having regained an upright posture, Charley glared in amazement at his leader and felt prompted to protest. His habit of whittling pieces of wood had brought the Maxim brothers to grief and he felt that he should do something to avenge them. If he did, they might forget how his innocent pastime had affected them.

"You mean you're letting that peckerwood bastard get away with it, Parson?" the young man squawked. "Hell! I'll——"

"Do like the Deacon tells you," the scout put in.

"Yeah?" Charley spat out, swinging to face the speaker and starting to raise his knife. "Who says so?"

"I do," answered the scout. "If you go ag'in that Texan with the knife, he's like to take it away from you and kill you——And if you don't turn it away from me, I'll lick him to doing it."

Suddenly Charley found himself looking at the barrel of the plainsman's gun. Beyond it was a tanned, cold, savage face which sent a chill of apprehension through the young hard-case. Charley had seen enough killers to know the signs. There stood a man as dangerous, or maybe more so,

as the worst of Wightman's band. The .36 calibre muzzle
of the Navy Colt appeared to have a bore the size of a
Napoleon cannon as it pointed at his head.

Almost grinding his teeth in rage and frustration,
Wightman forced himself to keep his temper in check.
Schooling his face into what, for him, passed as an expression of benevolent friendship, he spoke to the others.

"Peace, brothers. Let there be no more conflict between
us."

"If you say so, Parson," gritted Charley, not regretting
the chance to escape a showdown and returning his knife to
its sheath.

"Come, brothers," Wightman continued, promising
himself revenge of the most violent kind if the scout had
been lying about the presence of the Dragoons. "Let us
secure this evil sinner before he works more mischief on
us."

Seated on the floor of a stall in the small barn, hands
and feet securely tied with strong rope, Dusty felt a growing sense of apprehension and concern. Almost an hour
had gone by since he had been brought into the building.
So far neither the scout nor the guerillas had returned.

There had been no hope for Dusty to escape while being
escorted to the stall and fastened up. Nor could the scout
make a move to save him. Wightman, Charley Herbert and
Gustav had fanned in a circle around them, too far apart for
there to be any hope of jumping them collectively. Under
the circumstances, the scout had taken the only way out
and given cooperation to guerillas.

Give him full due, that long-haired Yankee sure knew
how to tie a man. Of course, there had been no other way
in which he could have acted while watched so closely by
the four guerillas. He had secured Dusty's wrists at the

rear, taking the end of the rope down to knot it on the loop about his thighs and connect to the fastenings about his ankles. Held in that manner, Dusty found the scout had left enough play on the vertical rope for him to sit in reasonable comfort. There was no way in which he could set himself free.

With the prisoner secured to his satisfaction, Wightman had led the others from the barn. Left to himself, Dusty rested his shoulders against the wall of the stall and let the effects of his exertions wear off. He thought of the information he had gathered outside Pine Buff and wondered if his men had managed to evade the Yankees and deliver the warning. If not, the rocket battery might inflict heavy and ruinous losses upon Ole Devil's already outnumbered Army of Arkansas and North Texas. It would not be a wild exaggeration to say that those losses might change the whole course of the War. Already the Union's superior economic and industrial facilities were swinging the balance in their favour. If Arkansas was lost, the Texans serving on other battle fronts would want to return and protect their home States. Even if they were compelled to remain with their commands, morale would be weakened.

Yet Dusty could do nothing about the situation at that moment. He knew better than to let a wave of despondency take control of him, for he would need all his wits about him if he hoped to escape. Should he not get away, he wondered what his fate might be.

Unless the scout accomplished something in the near future, both he and Dusty could have mighty short life-expectancies. As soon as the guerillas knew for sure that the long-haired Yankee had been bluffing, they would do their damndest to kill him. Possessing their superior numbers, they most likely would succeed. After which, it would be Dusty's turn. While he suspected that Wightman saw some benefit in keeping him alive, the Parson might not be able to hold back the vengeance-seeking brothers.

Slowly the barn's door opened and Dusty tensed. There was a surreptitious motion about the moving timbers which hinted that the man beyond them wished to avoid letting the hinges creak. Seated in the stall, Dusty tried to think how he might defend himself should whoever was coming be one of the guerillas sneaking in to avenge the injuries inflicted on his companions. That young cuss, Charley, might do it as a sop for the humiliation he had suffered at the scout's hands, or to placate the brothers' anger over the result of his discarding the so-useful stick.

Although Dusty knew of ways to protect himself while his hands were tied behind his back,* to put them into practice he needed to have the use of his legs and feet. Fastened in such a manner, there seemed little he could do.

Stepping into the barn, with a final glance at the cabin, the scout closed the door. Dusty let out a deep breath of relief. Going by the fact that his gunbelt dangled from the Yankee's left hand, he concluded that the time to escape had come. Crossing to the stall, the scout hung the gunbelt on its wall. Then he drew the knife from its boot-top sheath. While cutting Dusty's bonds, he spoke in a soft, conspiratory manner.

"Sorry I couldn't get here sooner, Cap'n. That blasted Charley was stuck to me like a burr to a blanket. Sort of took a shine to me, way he was talking—and how he talked. Hey, you sure worked them three over good, they're only just about getting on their feet again and won't feel like going a-dancing at a ball for a fair spell."

"I sure tried to get 'em that way." Dusty answered,

---

*One example of this is given in *Goodnight's Dream*.

working his arms and feet as the circulation pulsed back through them.

"Happen you're up to it," said the scout, helping Dusty to rise. "Buckle on your belt. We may still have to fight our way out of here."

"Sure," Dusty agreed.

Never had the leather of the gunbelt felt so comforting as it did as Dusty swung it about his waist. Swiftly he coupled up the belt buckle with its 'CSA' embossment, then knotted the pigging tongs about his thighs. After flexing his fingers a few times, finding them working with their usual fluid ease, he drew and examined the Colts one at a time. Realising how the gesture might appear to the scout, Dusty turned in his direction. The tanned face, framed by the long tawny hair, showed only complete agreement with what had been an involuntary but understandable precaution.

"I've got my horses 'n' that black of your'n down by the corral, Cap'n," commented the scout. "That jasper you downed's lucky. If you hadn't stopped him, it'd've likely stomped his head down level with his shoulders."

"What's our play?" Dusty wanted to know.

"Be best if we pull out sneaky-like. I'll fetch some soldiers along here and tend to their needings."

Something in the scout's tone brought Dusty's gaze back to his face. There was a tight-lipped grimness which added fuel to the small Texan's earlier suspicions about the condition of the farm.

"What happened to the folks who own this place?"

"Those bastards killed 'em," replied the scout coldly. "Man, his wife 'n' two children. I found a tin-type of 'em and that young bastard come a-bragging to me's how they'd shot 'em all 'n' planted 'em in the hawg-pens. Lord!

I don't know how I kept from blowing his head off 's he stood."

"Buller's not known for bothering what happens to our civilians," Dusty pointed out. "If he doesn't get them, I'll fetch my Company over here and we will."

"Sooner we go, better our chances of getting clear to do it," the scout suggested. "Let's go. Given just a mite of luck, we'll be mounted up and off afore they know it."

That "mite" of good fortune was not to be granted to them.

Walking from the barn side by side, the escaping pair found themselves confronted by—from right to left—Gustav, Wightman, Herbert and Charley. Slamming to a halt as if they had walked into an invisible wall, the guerillas glared in a mixture of shock, amazement and anger at the small Texan and the tall, long-haired Yankee scout. Of the six men only Gustav, carrying his rifle at what soldiers termed the "high-port" position, held a weapon in his hands.

At first Parson Wightman had been too busy attempting to calm the partially-recovered Maxim brothers to notice the scout's departure. Even when, on being questioned, Charley admitted that the scout had left to take his horses to the corral, the guerilla leader did not appreciate the full implications straight away. An uneasy suspicion began to gnaw at him when he remembered that the Rebel captain's Colt-loaded gunbelt had been hanging across the scout's saddle.

Feeling distinctly uneasy, Wightman had gathered Herbert, Gustav and Charley together. The Maxim brothers had retired to the main bedroom, nursing their hurts and telling each other what they would do with the Texan. Wanting men on whom he could rely for instant obedience,

Wightman had not called them. Instead he led the other three from the cabin. With Blocky and Abel not yet returned, Wightman wished to avoid a confrontation with the scout. So he ordered his companions to keep their weapons holstered, but allowed Gustav to carry along the Sharps rifle.

Coming face to face with the scout and the Rebel captain handed all four men a bad shock. Wightman felt it more than the other three. All the vicious, barely controllable temper that had cost him his hopes of a bishopric boiled up in a seething blast.

At last Wightman knew for sure that he had been tricked. The scout's actions proved that no Troop of Dragoons were following on his trail. Instead, he had lied to save his neck—and to keep them from laying hands on the hated Secessionist.

On a *Secessionist* scum!

Why would any *Yankee* scout take such a desperate chance to save an enemy?

In his almost maniacal thrust of fury, Wightman sprang to what appeared to be the only answer.

That was no scout employed by the Union Army, but a Confederate spy in disguise. A lousy, stinking peckerwood agent, clad in the dress of a Federal supporter. There could be no other explanation—and only one way to treat the answer.

"Cursed be all traitors!" Parson Wightman bellowed, reaching for his gun; an example followed by his three companions.

Down lashed two guerilla hands, while a third went from right to left, and Gustav tried to bring his rifle into line.

Starting at the same instant, Dusty and the scout commenced their draws. Flashing across, Dusty's hands curled around the bone handles of his Army Colts. Turning palms outwards, the scout wrapped his fingers about the ivory grips of his matched Navies. The .44 calibre revolvers cleared Dusty's holsters slightly ahead of the .36 handguns leaving the long-haired scout's silk sash. Swinging into alignment at waist level, Dusty's weapons made a single crash; to be echoed by the lighter, more ragged twin bark of his companion's armament.

Hit twice in the head, Wightman fell with his Navy Colt still not clear of leather. Caught in the withering blast of gunfire, the man to his right and left sides joined him in crashing to the ground.

Stunned by the shattering holocaust of doom that had ripped into his companions, Charley froze with his gun barely above the lip of his holster. He wanted to scream for mercy, but the chance to do so did not come. Cocking his guns as their barrels rose and fell, the scout turned the right hand weapon and squeezed its trigger. The 140 grains of conical lead spiked into Charley's throat and ripped apart his jugular vein. Gagging hoarsely, the young man spun around. Blood spurted from the ruptured flesh as he tumbled across the bodies of Herbert and Wightman.

"Come on!" Dusty snapped. "Let's go, *pron——!*"

Flying from the direction of the cabin, a bullet spun the hat from the scout's head. As they started to swivel around, Dusty and the scout saw the three Maxim brothers fanning out from the house. Stap had fired the shot, aiming it at Dusty. With his eyes swollen to two puffy slits by the small Texan's earlier attack, the youngest brother could not line his sights as well as usual; especially when he wanted to shoot in a hurry. So his lead missed its mark and warned their prospective victim of the danger.

Alerted to the brothers' presence, Dusty and the scout realised which of them would be the greatest danger.

Swaying slightly, for the effects of the stick's impact on his temple had not fully departed, Aaron flung a twin-bar-relled, ten-gauge shotgun to his shoulder. Hobbling pain-fully and suffering a sensation like having two red-hot six-pounder cannonballs between his thighs, Job brought up a Sharps carbine. Each of the weapons slanted in Dusty's direction.

Seeing that he had been selected as the mark for both brothers, Dusty flung himself away from the scout. He saw the brothers trying to correct their alignment, then flame and smoke burst from their weapons. With an ear-splitting crack, the carbine's heavy-calibre bullet passed a foot above Dusty's head. An instant later, he heard the sibilant hissing as buckshot balls went by. In later years, Dusty would always swear that three of the shotgun's nine .32 pellets made a triangle around his upper body.

So intent were the brothers on avenging themselves upon the man who had caused them severe grief that they ignored the scout. Left free from their attentions, he took full advantage of his chances. Right, left, right, left. Four times his Navy Colts spat, held at shoulder level so that he could use their sights. What excellent purpose he put them to showed as Aaron stumbled and dropped the carbine, while Job twisted in a circle, sending the charge from the second barrel harmlessly into the side of the cabin. Bleed-ing from a hole in his chest and another between the eyes, Job crumpled like a pole-axed steer. Clutching at his stom-ach, with agony twisting his surly features into hideous lines, Aaron sank to his knees.

Oblivious to his brother's fate, Stap plunged towards Dusty. Three times the younger brother's revolver banged, but without any bullet taking effect. Thinking of the mur-dered family, Dusty did not hesitate with his response. Ramming down his forward foot, he brought himself to a stop. Lifting to waist level, the Army Colts bellowed an answer to Spat's challenge. Dusty shot the only way possible under the circumstances, to obtain an instant kill—and he succeeded admirably. Where Spat's eyes had been, two gaping holes blossomed as if by magic. A corpse hurtled through the air for a moment before landing on its back.

Still Aaron was not finished. Knowing that he must die a painful death, he made a final attempt to take at least one of his enemies with him. Withdrawing his gore-smeared right hand, he clawed the revolver from its holster. Before he could use it, two balls from the scout's Navy Colts struck him in the head.

"That finished them," said the scout, returning his weapons to the silk sash. "We might's well move off."

"Just might as well," Dusty agreed and holstered his Colts.

They turned just in time. With their thoughts fixed on the same matter, they had almost forgotten that two other members of the guerilla band remained alive and at liberty. Looking over the corral, with the three waiting horses, at the slope, they received an unpleasant reminder.

Returning with the news that no soldiers were in the vicinity, Abel Maxim and Blocky had heard the shooting. So they had left their horses ground-hitched and, rifles in hand, advanced on foot. They had come on the scene too late to save any of their companions, or to take the Texan and the scout by surprise.

"Get 'em!" Blocky yelled, dropping his right knee to the ground and thrusting the Spencer's butt against his right shoulder.

Being armed with a muzzle-loading Mississippi rifle, Abel elected to remain on his feet. By doing so, he could reload much faster than when kneeling or prone. Unlike his brothers, he did not allow hatred of the small Rebel to override common sense. Nor did Blocky. They selected the most dangerous target and at that moment it was not the grey-uniformed captain.

With the two guerillas something like a hundred and fifty yards away, the scout knew his Navy Colts were of no use. So he flung himself forward, racing in a zigzag course to where his Henry rifle swung in its boot from the dun gelding's saddle.

Watching the two men on the rim, Dusty guessed at their intentions. Instead of following the scout, he sent his left hand flashing across to draw its Colt and dropped to the ground. Breaking his fall with his right hand, he lowered his stomach until it rested on the soil. Pointing his body directly at the target, he extended both arms and placed his right hand under the Colt's butt. With his chin resting on the left deltoid muscle, his left eye looked along the outstretched gun-arm. It was a position permitting a man with Dusty's ability to shoot accurately almost to the longest limits of the revolver's load. Like the guerillas, he made his choice of target on the basis of which man posed the greater threat.

Pressing the trigger Dusty felt the Colt's recoil-kick tilt the barrel upwards. Through the swirling powder smoke, he saw the hat jerk off Blocky's head. Coming so unexpectedly, the bullet made the man rock backwards in alarm just as his forefinger carried the Spencer's trigger to the firing position. The heavy repeating rifle bellowed, but its barrel slanted into the air. Caught by the recoil thrust, Blocky over-balanced. Dropping his weapon, he threw his hands behind him to lessen the force of his fall.

On Abel's Mississippi rifle banging, a hank of tawny hair flew from the left side of the scout's head. Only the fact that he was taking rapid evasive action saved him from a worse injury. Plunging forward the last few feet, he grabbed the wrist of the Henry's butt. A jerk tore the medicine boot free and, swinging the rifle to the right, he flung the buckskin covering from it. With that done, he snapped the weapon towards the firing position.

"Load it!" Dusty roared, suddenly remembering that he had emptied the Henry's chamber that morning.

After shooting, Abel dropped the rifle's butt to the ground. He had come to the rim ready for trouble, having collected his powder horn and bullet-pouch from his saddlebags on hearing the commotion at the farm. While reaching for the horn, he saw the effect of Dusty's long-range shot. Showing no interest in Blocky's welfare, Abel let the muzzle-loader fall and snatched up the metal-cartridge repeater. Hooking his fingers into the trigger-guard-lever, he thrust it down to eject the empty cartridge case.

Hearing Dusty's yell, the scout understood its meaning. In a blurring movement, he sent the mechanism through its loading cycle and took his aim. Twice the Henry spurted white puffs of powder smoke, the lever flicking down and up between the detonations. On each discharge, Abel's body jolted. The Spencer's barrel sank downwards. Stumbling around in a circle, the last of the brothers passed over the rim and came rolling down the slope.

Twirling himself around, Blocky rump-bounced out of sight of the two men by the buildings. Once sure they could not lay their sights on him, he rose and ran to the waiting horses. Swinging afork his mount, he grabbed the reins of Abel's. Riding the animals in a half circle, he headed away from the valley as fast as he could make them run.

"I'd say that's the last," Dusty remarked, standing up and holstering his Colt.

"And good riddance to 'em," the scout replied, lowering the Henry.

"We'd best just go and make sure none of them're left alive," Dusty suggested as the scout collected his medicine boot.

With his Henry once more hanging from the dun's saddle, the scout accompanied Dusty around the bodies. And bodies they were, for not one of Wightman's band—except for the fleeing Blocky—remained alive.

Returning to their horses, Dusty and the scout looked at each other. They each had the same thought in mind again and this time the scout put it into words.

"Which of us's who's prisoner now, Cap'n?"

There, if either of them cared to force the issue, was a mighty tough point. While their experience when faced by Wightman and the three guerillas had proved Dusty to be the faster on the draw, both knew that he could not get off a shot in time to prevent the scout from throwing lead at him. So, should they make a face-to-face issue of it, both might easily be killed.

That point aside, each had saved the other's life at least twice since they first met. Their eyes met and each knew that the other felt they should forget the War at that moment. Maybe they would meet on the field of battle in the future, but that would be different. Right now there was too much between them for either to desire the other dead or a captive.

"What say we call it a stand-off?" Dusty suggested. "We'll go our ways and figure we'd never met."

"I'm for that," enthused the scout and offered his right hand. "Know something, Cap'n? I don't know your name."

"Dusty Fog," the small Texan introduced, shaking hands. "And I don't know your's."

"It's James Butler Hickok," answered the scout. "Only that's a mite fancy. Folks mostly call me 'Wild Bill.'"

Author's Note

Dusty and Hickok did not meet again on the field of battle. Having no desire to do so, the scout had reported to Buller's headquarters in Little Rock and announced his intention of returning to the East to rejoin his pard, California Bill. With other things on their mind, Buller's staff raised no objections. In the years that followed, Dusty's and Hickok's paths would cross; but the scout ensured that their interests never clashed.

Kiowa and Vern Hassle reached their destinations in safety, delivering the warnings. Then they rejoined their captain, who had also made good his escape from the Union-held territory. Dusty had called the play correctly in his assumption that the "tin-clads" would be the rocket battery's first objectives. Due to the warning they had received, the riverboats were ready to counter such an attack. On its meeting with the Georgia, the battery's commanding officer went ahead with his preconceived plot. Expecting the Rebel's ship's crew to mistake his men for a cavalry patrol, he had given the order to go into action. The captain of the Georgia had identified the battery and proved to have taken precautions. At some expense in sweat and effort, improvised mountings had been fitted so that all four Williams Rapid Fire cannon could be carried on the side facing the Yankees' bank of the river. Each gun had a crew capable of producing its maximum rate of sixty-five one-pound, 1.75 inch rounds a minute. Caught in a hail of such fire, the battery's commander died and it suffered heavy losses in men and horses. After taking such a mauling, the remnants of the ill-fated outfit were sent East to refit. It was equipped with cannon instead of rockets, and never returned to the Arkansas battle front.

PART TWO

A Convention of War

One o'clock in the morning!

After an hour on sentry duty, Private Alberto Genaro stood and glowered bitterly at the distant, unlit rows of tents. Beneath their shelter, most other members of his field artillery battery would be sleeping in as much comfort as they could devise while bivouacked on the hard Arkansas countryside. Even the rest of the guard, with the exception of Dutchy Kruger over by the horse-lines, were almost certainly wrapped in their blankets and snoring like pigs.

Not poor old Genaro though.

He had to stand his guard between midnight and four a.m.; the most miserable and depressing tour of duty any soldier ever faced.

Hell! It all seemed so damned pointless, too.

Earlier in the night, the lights of Little Rock could have

been seen glowing, a mile to the south at most, beyond the valley of the Arkansas River. By continuing their journey for another ninety minutes or so, the battery could have been bedded down in comfort and with solid roofs above their heads. Instead of pushing on, Captain Luxton had insisted that they halted before sundown and made camp in the open air.

So then what had happened?

Poor old Genaro, armed with a short artillery sword and a Springfield carbine, wound up roaming among the parked vehicles and pieces of the battery during the part of the night when all sensible people were in bed.

Performing his duty under the prevailing conditions struck Genaro as both stupid and futile. Between the battery's current location and the Ouachita River—with the Rebels over on its western bank—lay a good eighty miles of Union-held territory. In the unlikely event of a Confederate cavalry patrol penetrating so far, they would be disinclined to concern themselves with a field artillery battery's six 12-powder gun-howitzers, caissons, limbers, battery-wagon and travelling forge. With the Arkansas, Saline and Ouachita Rivers to cross before reaching safety, the grey-clad raiders would search for loot of greater portability.

So, to Genaro's way of thinking, there was no danger to the battery and walking the guard served only to deprive him of well-earned rest. There could not, he concluded as he leaned his carbine against the wheel of a Napoleon and fumbled in his pockets for a cigarette, possibly be any Rebels closer than the disarmed population of Little Rock.

Which only was to prove how little Genaro knew of the true state of affairs in his immediate vicinity.

Having left their horses in the care of their companions a full mile to the north, Captain Dustine Edward Marsden

Fog of the Texas Light Cavalry and his Company's sergeant major now crouched in a hollow not more than thirty feet from the disinterested Yankee sentry.

Moving in on foot through the darkness, they had taken advantage of Genaro's indifferent patrol to crawl that close undetected. Concealed in the shallow depression, they knew that approaching any nearer without being located would be difficult, if not impossible. Then, as if wishing to assist the Confederate cause, the Yankee artilleryman had obligingly presented them with an opportunity of silencing him. The watching Rebels could be counted on to make the most of such a chance.

Lean as a poorly-nourished beanpole, Sergeant Major Billy Jack topped a six foot length with close-cropped black hair and a thin, careworn, anxious cast of features above a prominent Adam's apple. He presented such a lugubrious appearance that the first sight of the "V"-shaped triple bars and arc of silk denoting his rank came as a surprise. Bareheaded, he wore a cadet-grey, waist-long tunic and tight, yellow-striped breeches ending in knee-high boots. Around his middle hung a wide gunbelt carrying two walnut-handled 1860 Army Colts in open-topped holsters tied low to his thighs. In his hands, he held a fifty-foot length of three-strand, hard-plaited Manila rope specially prepared for his needs.

At Billy Jack's side lay a young man fast building a name for himself on the Arkansas battlefront; first coming into prominence by his bravery and ability while leading a cavalry charge that many of the combantants claimed had turned the course of the battle at Mark's Mill in the South's favor.

As yet the Yankees did not know Dusty Fog so well as they would come to when he attended a Federal court-martial to give evidence on behalf of a Union Army lieutenant falsely accused of cowardice.* To save Lieutenant Kirby Cogshill's life,† Dusty Fog would have to endanger his own and would be compelled to kill General Buller in a duel the commander of the Union Army of Arkansas forced upon him. Then Dusty would so bedevil Buller's successor that General Horace Trumpeter would place a bounty on the young Texan's head with tragic—and for the general, fatal—results.‡

To the Union Army in Arkansas, Dusty Fog would become synonymous with raiding, losses of urgently-needed equipment and supplies, or other similar forms of military disaster. He would also be known as a gallant, chivalrous enemy of great courage, integrity and efficiency.

Already Confederate sympathisers from the Lone Star State were boasting of his qualities of leadership. At a young eighteen, those qualities had won him the rank of captain—awarded in the field at Mark's Mill—and placed him in command of the Texas Light Cavalry's hard-riding, harder-fighting Company "C." Never slow to glorify prominent sons of their state, the Texans told of how Dusty Fog could draw his revolvers in blinding speed and throw lead with great accuracy from them; or mentioned proudly that he possessed the bare-handed fighting skill to lick any man in either Army.

What kind of man inspired such claims at so early an age?

Curly, dusty-blond hair topped a face that was handsome—though not in an eye-catching manner—tanned, showed strength of will, intelligence and an air of com-

*Told in the "The Futility of War" episode of *The Fastest Gun in Texas*.
†How Cogshill repaid Dusty is told in *Cuchilo*.
‡Told in *Kill Dusty Fog!*

manding attention. Tight-rolled and knotted about his throat, a scarlet silk bandana trailed long ends down the front of his tunic. Copied from a style originated by a 1st Lieutenant Mark Counter*—with whom Dusty would one day be closely associated†—the tunic continued the bandana's defiance of the *Manual of Dress Regulations*. Its stand-up collar carried the conventional triple three-inch long, half-inch wide gold bars of his rank. Two rows of seven buttons each graced its double-breasted front and its sleeves bore above their yellow cuffs the double, gold braid, Austrian knot "chicken-guts" device by which the Confederate States' Army further identified its captains. No skirt extended halfway between hip and knee as *Regulations* required. His riding breeches and boots did conform to *Regulations*, but his weapon belt departed from them. Like Billy Jack's, it rode lower than the official pattern, possessed no means of carrying a sabre, and had open-topped holsters cut to leave the trigger-guards of the revolvers exposed. However, the matched bone-handled Army Colts rode butt forward instead of pointing to the rear.

All in all, Dusty Fog's wide shoulders and lean waist conveyed an impression of exceptional muscular power and strength. Despite the fact that his height was barely five foot six, none of his Company—and few others who came into contact with the force of his personality—ever thought of him as being small.

Studying the sentry for a few seconds, Dusty addressed his sergeant major in a whisper.

"Reckon you can rope him from here?"

"Likely not," Billy Jack answered dismally, but no

*Mark Counter's history is told in the author's floating outfit stories.
†How and why this came about is told in *The Ysabel Kid*.

louder. "I'll certain-sure miss. Then he'll holler 'n' wake the whole boiling of 'em 'n' we'll both of us get catched, or killed."

Which meant, as Dusty knew well, that Billy Jack considered the chances of silencing the indolent sentry to be greatly in their favour. For all his doleful appearance and constant predictions of doom, the lean sergeant major was a fighting man from soda to hock* and well-deserving of his rank. Knowing the risks involved, and what his commanding officer hoped to do, he would not attempt to rope the Yankee soldier unless almost certain of success.

Measuring with his eyes the distance separating him from Genaro, Billy Jack carefully made his preparations. The Yankee soldier was standing with his back to the Texans' position, shoulders hunched and hands gathered about the match he was using to light his cigarette. In such a posture, he could not be caught as Billy Jack knew must be done. Waiting for his chance, the lanky Texan worked the stem of his rope through the two-inch long, rawhide-wrapped eye of the *honda* to increase the size of the loop he would use when the time came.

With his cigarette glowing, Genaro leaned against the Napoleon's barrel. Resting his arms on top of the cold metal of the tube, he kept his head held up so as to observe the tent lines and see if the officer-of-the-day appeared to make the rounds. City-born and not long enlisted, Genaro lacked the country-dwellers' keen sense of a veteran's natural alertness. So he failed to hear certain faint sounds that ought to have warned him of danger.

Slowly Billy Jack eased himself upright and from the hollow. There could be no extensive twirling of the rope as an aid to accuracy, its noise might alarm the sentry. How-

*Soda and hock: the first and last cards in a deck used for playing faro.

ever, the lean, miserable Rebel's repertoire of roping methods offered a solution to that problem. Ensuring that the stem, or spoke, of the rope—that part not forming the loop—could move freely, he prepared to make his throw.

One quick whirl before him carried the rope up to the right and above his head. Then the loop and spoke flew through the air. Deft hands turned the loop to flatten horizontally before it reached its victim. Sliding along the stem as it advanced, the *honda* decreased the size of the loop. Passing downwards around Genaro's kepi, the reduced noose scraped by his ears and came to rest on his shoulders.

Called a hooley-anne throw, the method used by Billy Jack was a head-catch originally designed to collect a horse from a bunch in a corral without disturbing the rest of them. It proved equally effective when used against another human being.

Wasting no time in self-congratulation over a masterly piece of roping, Billy Jack tugged sharply on the stem between his hands. Before Genaro could respond to the unexpected assault, the rope snapped tight about his throat. Jerked backwards, unable to cry out or snatch up his carbine, the artilleryman lost his footing and sat down hard. Deprived of one weapon, the impact of his landing caused him to forget his other. It would also have driven the air from his lungs, but the constricting coil about his throat prevented that from happening.

Moving closer, Billy Jack swung his hands in a circular motion. Curling away from him, the stem of the rope passed over Genaro's head. Even as the Yankee decided to make a grab for the strangling loop, a coil of Manila settled around his biceps and torso. With his arms effectively pinned and helpless, Genaro could do no more than sit and listen to the sound of footsteps approaching from his rear.

No mean hand with a catch-rope himself. Dusty had watched his companion in silent admiration. Dusty had often heard it claimed that the only thing Billy Jack could not do with a rope was make it stand upright, climb to the top and sit on the *honda*. There were times when Dusty felt his lanky sergeant major could even accomplish *that*.

Slipping a specially-manufactured gag from his breeches' pocket, Dusty ran towards Genaro. Made of a hard ball of rubber, encased in rawhide and fitted with two cords, it could be rapidly attached to a captive and effectively prevented him from making any outcry.

Catching hold of the dazed, half-stranged artilleryman's shoulder, Dusty inserted the ball between his open lips. Acting with a speed that permitted Genaro no opportunity of resisting, the small Texan affixed the cords. Drawing them tight, he knotted them behind the Yankee's head.

Billy Jack produced two rawhide "piggin' strings," of the kind used to secure hogs or calves, from inside his tunic. With the gagging completed, he turned Genaro face-downwards. Loosening the stem's coil a little, Billy Jack drew the Yankee's wrists together. Lashing them in a way that would require a knife to set them free, the Texan repeated the process on Genaro's ankles. With that done, he removed the strangling loop and stood back coiling his rope.

"Nice work, Billy Jack," Dusty praised quietly. "We've got him safe enough."

"Sure never thought we'd do it," the sergeant major replied dolefully. "I'll bet he busts loose and gets the drop on us."

"Damned if I shouldn't've picked a turkey-buzzard,"*

---

* Turkey-buzzard: Cathartes Aura, the American Turkey Vulture.

Dusty grinned, "instead of a whip-poor-will for you to use as a signal."

"I allus see more of 'em around me than 'whips'," Billy Jack answered. "So I'd know how to do one better."

While carrying on their whispered conversation, the two Texans had been scrutinising the surrounding area with eyes and ears. Alert to detect any hint that their presence had been discovered, they saw and heard nothing to alarm them. Cupping his hands to his mouth, Billy Jack gave a passable impersonation of a whip-poor-will's plaintive call.

"That was so real," Dusty declared. "I'll bet every lil gal 'whip' around'll be headed this way."

"Sure," agreed Jack miserably. "And I know what they'll do when they fly over me. They nev——"

The remainder of his mournful tirade went unsaid as the call received an answer from the vicinity of the battery's horse-lines.

Although he might have given an argument on the matter, Private "Dutchy" Kruger should have counted himself a very fortunate man. Caught asleep at his post by two men who had small regard for the sanctity of an enemy's life, he had Dusty Fog to thank that he received nothing worse than a blow on the head from a revolver's butt. Stunned, but still alive, he lay face down on the ground and received the same treatment as that given to Genaro.

Instinctively Dusty Fog knew that the morale effect of taking sentries alive and leaving them bound, gagged, but unharmed, was far greater than killing them. So he had given his scouts orders to that effect. With men of less ability than that possessed by Sergeant Kiowa Cotton and Corporal Vern Hassle, Dusty would never have issued such dangerously prohibitive instructions. It said much for the respect in which they held their youthful commanding officer that the two hard-bitten scouts had troubled to carry out the far-from-easy directive.

Experts in their trade, schooled under the exacting conditions of Indian warfare, they had experienced little difficulty in stalking and clubbing down the lethargic Kruger as he sat sleeping with his back to a tree's trunk. Their harder task was still to come.

Sergeant Cotton could not be termed handsome. Tall, lean, black-haired, he had a face that in time of stress resembled that of a particularly mean, blood-thirsty Indian. Even when relaxed, he would not be considered any oil-painting. He wore an untidy uniform, a battered campaign hat with an eagle's feather stuck in its band, while a Remington Army revolver and a bowie knife dangled from his belt.

Kneeling by the unconscious Yankee and attending to fastening a gag in his mouth, Kiowa grinned wolfishly at his companion. If his flowing white hair was any proof, Corporal Vern Hassle had seen many years of life. Yet he moved with an agility a younger man might have envied and his eyes flickered keenly in a seamed, lined old face.

"There's Billy Jack," Hassle breathed as the call of a whip-poor-will reached their ears.

"Best finish hawg-tying this *hombre,*" Kiowa replied. "Then we'll let Cap'n Dusty know we've done it."

"Sounds like Kiowa and Vern've got the horse-guard," Dusty commented as Hassle answered the signal.

"Or he got them," countered Billy Jack. "And now he's doing the 'whip' to trick us. Don't see why we should be the only 'n's fool enough to be catched."

Completing his speech, the sergeant major repeated the same type of bird's call three times in succession. Off in the darkness to the north, another member of the Company replied.

While awaiting the arrival of reinforcements, Dusty walked over and boarded the nearest limber. Raising the lid of its chest, he looked inside. The light of the stars and new moon was sufficient for him to identify the contents and know that the chest carried its full load. Its eight compartments held thirty-two 12-pounder rounds, two spare cartridges, seventy-five friction primers, three portfires and one-and-a-half yards of slow match.

From his position, Dusty counted the remaining vehicles. Each cannon had its own limber and caisson, the former carrying one and the latter three ammunition chests. Being a battery newly-arrived from the East, each of the chests ought to carry its full complement of equipment. Even if they did not, there was sufficient material on hand for what he planned; especially as the six reserve caissons stood in a line behind the others. Beyond them was the battery-wagon containing—if fully loaded—oil, paint, spare gunners' tools, stocks and spokes, over two hundred pounds of reserve harness, axes, spades and picks. At its side was the travelling-forge, with blacksmiths' tools, spare hardware and iron, as well as 300 pounds of ready-shaped horseshoes and nails. A replacement battery, on its way to join the Union's Army of Arkansas, could be expected to come fully equipped.

The loss would be that much greater, if its destruction could be effected.

Concluding his examination of the battery's material,* Dusty gave a disgusted grunt. Whoever commanded it

---

* Material: in Artillery terms, the battery's guns, vehicles and equipment as opposed to its personnel and horses.

must be very inexperienced, incompetent, criminally negligent, or a permutation of the three, to camp with so few precautions even that close to Little Rock. The lax behaviour, however, did not entirely come as a surprise to the small Texan.

Wanting to strike down the heart of the Confederate States, Federal policy demanded that the pick of their troops be reserved for the Eastern and Southern battle fronts. General Buller had a few good outfits under his command—Verncombe's 6th "New Jersey" Dragoons for instance. Mostly the commanding general in Arkansas had to make do with regiments produced by merging several disrupted privately-formed Volunteer battalions, recuperating from losses in action, or found wanting under the harsh tests of combat. Badly-led, poorly-trained demoralised, such regiments made the work of the Confederate States' cavalry far easier to accomplish in the Toothpick State.

Taking a round from the chest, Dusty dropped to the ground and crossed to the nearest Napoleon. By manipulating the elevating screw, he raised the breech of the barrel. Resting the metal ball of the round on the cheek of the carriage, he lowered the barrel and held it firmly in place. He had just fixed the demolition charge into position when twenty men of his Company arrived. On hearing Billy Jack's signal, they have moved in silently and were ready to play their part in depriving the Yankees of a field artillery battery. Having previously visualised how he would handle such a situation, Dusty had already instructed his men in the duties they were to perform.

Courage in action alone did not account for Dusty's success as a military raider. When setting out on a mission, he always tried to carry along items that would be of use. One commodity he never left behind was quick-match fuses and his reinforcements held sufficient for their needs. Swiftly, silently, the Texans fanned out to attend to their appointed tasks.

It was hard, exacting and nerve-wracking work that demanded the utmost in concentration on the part of the men carrying it out. Not fifty yards from the rear vehicles, the members of the battery lay sleeping in their tents. Any undue noise would rouse the Yankees, who, by weight of numbers, would drive off the Texans and waste the work already carried out.

About to lift out a round, one of the Texans saw the lid of the chest slip and fall. By inserting his fingers, he prevented the bang of wood against wood and he bit on his bottom lip to prevent his pain-induced curses from becoming audible.

Working in the battery-wagon, another man dislodged an axe. Hearing the brief clatter it made, the whole party froze. Full thirty seconds dragged by before Dusty felt satisfied that the sound had not disturbed the sleeping Yankee artillerymen and gave the signal for the work to continue.

Joined by half-a-dozen assistants, the pick of a Company noted for its expert horsemen, Kiowa Cotton and Vern Hassle set about a no less demanding and equally important duty. Selecting and dominating mounts for their own use, with the need for silence of paramount importance, was no work for the inexperienced. With that task accomplished, they gave their attention to the rest of the battery's horses. In addition to setting the animals free, Kiowa's section had to silently curb any attempt to stray or prematurely quit the severed picket lines.

Held immobile by his bonds, although Billy Jack had thoughtfully turned him onto his back, Genaro strained his eyes and ears in an attempt to discover what the Texans were doing. He could see and hear little, but what he did told him all that he needed to know.

Each of the remaining five Napoleons had a round of ammunition fixed where the two-and-a-half pound powder firing-charge would do the most damage. The battery-wagon and the travelling forge both received the contents of one chest from the nearest caissons to ensure their demolition.

While his men worked, Dusty gave thought to the detonating of the charges. Quick-match, made of cotton-yarn impregnated with a highly-combustible compound, burned at a rate of a yard in thirteen seconds when exposed to the open air. Composed of three lightly-twisted strands of hemp, flax or cotton rope, slow-match required an hour to consume four-and-a-half inches. By combining the qualities of the two, Dusty hoped to strike the essential happy medium between allowing his men to withdraw in safety and permitting sufficient time to elapse for the raid to be discovered before the explosions took place.

"We'll give them a yard of quick-match, Billy Jack," Dusty decided, "and fasten a couple of inches of slow-match to it."

"Yo!" the sergeant major answered, giving the traditional cavalry response of assent. *"Two* inches?"

"We won't be starting it off from the end," Dusty assured him.

Using a piece of priming-wire found in a limber's chest, the sergeant major made a hole in the paper container of the round and through the close-textured flannel cartridge bag. Carefully he eased one end of a yard-length of quick match into the cavity so that it was buried in the powder. Extending the remainder of the fuse along the stock of the Napoleon, he knotted it to a piece of slow-match and looped them around the cannon's upper *prolonge* hook.

A cartridge in each limber's chest and the central chest of every caisson received a similar treatment, as did one of the rounds placed in the battery-wagon and the travelling-forge. At last everything was fused, ready and waiting for the fire that would start off the train of devastation.

Kept silent by his gag Genaro felt a growing sensation of alarm as the significance of his position became apparent to him. Often he had contended to his companions that he came from a long line of civilians and would be over-joyed when he went back to them. Impressed by the silence and grim, deadly purpose with which his captors worked he decided that his return was long overdue. A man stood but little chance of going home to marry his *amante* and raise many *bambinos* if he fought against such terrible people.

Given the good fortune to survive through the night, Genaro swore that he would take the first opportunity to set off home and chance being shot as a deserter. Not that, he told himself glumly, he could see much hope of his living through the night. Bound and helpless, unable to move, he would be blown up in company with the battery's material.

Making a tour of his party, Dusty checked that every-thing was ready. In passing he gave each man his orders.

"When Billy Jack gives the 'whip's' call, count to ten slowly. Then set off the slow-match about half-an-inch from the knot. No closer, but not much farther away. Light up a smoke ready to get things going."

One of the qualities that endeared Dusty to his men was that he gave orders, but did not add unnecessary warnings. Some officers would have emphasised that care must be taken to avoid letting the lighting-up process be seen by the Yankees. Knowing his party to be veterans and not in the least suicidally-inclined, Dusty figured he could count on them not to make foolish mistakes. On receiving his orders, each man turned his back to the tent lines, shielded the match's flame in his hands, and lit either a cigarette or a cigar.

Pausing only long enough for the man he addressed to whisper a confirmatory "Yo!", Dusty continued to the next member of his company and repeated his instructions. On rejoining Billy Jack, Dusty took one of the cigars lit by the sergeant major and blew its end to a rich, clear glow. From his place on the ground, Genaro saw ruddy glints like so many fireflies as Dusty's men crouched ready for the signal. At a nod from Dusty, Billy Jack once more sounded the call of a whip-poor-will.

"One!" Dusty counted.

"Two!" hissed the man by the tailgate of the battery-wagon.

"Three!" timed the soldier in the centre of the third reserve caisson.

"Four! Five!" said the tall, slim, debonair Sergeant Lou Bixby, thinking of times when he had counted the fall of trump cards in a high-stake whist game, but concentrating on the fuse leading into the number four gun's limber's chest.

"*Sei!*" thought Genaro, having heard Dusty's instructions and involuntarily counting off the seconds in his native Italian. "*Sette!*"

"Eight!" decided the corporal charged with the destruction of the travelling forge.

"Nine!" Billy Jack announced, in a whisper that held nothing of his usual dolorous tones.

"Ten!" Dusty concluded.

Laying the glowing tip of the borrowed cigar against the slow-match at the required distance from the knot connecting it to its faster-burning contemporary, Dusty watched it splutter into life. Once lit, only water, or smothering pressure, would halt the creeping fire. With an almost leisurely, yet deliberate spreading motion, the tiny red glow crept on its way.

Allowing for variations in the pace of each individual count and the fuses' rate of consumption, Dusty estimated that his men had between five-and-a-half and six-and-a-half minutes in which to get clear of the danger area. Already the other members of his party were converging upon him.

In a muck-sweat of anxiety, Genaro tried to burst his bonds. If the stories he had heard were true, the Rebels would leave him to his fate. In which case, he could do nothing to save himself. The gag in his mouth even prevented him from pleading for his life.

"Move out!" Dusty ordered and pointed swiftly to some of his men. "You four, tote this *hombre* with you!"

To his amazement and relief, Genaro felt himself gripped and raised from the ground between four of the Texans. Big, strong men, they carried the dumpy Italian soldier without difficulty. Maybe their holds were not gentle, but to Genaro it felt as if he were riding on a featherbed. Bearing the artilleryman between them, the quartet strode off at a fast pace on the heels of their companions.

"You too," Dusty growled at Billy Jack.

"Don't be too long," the sergeant major answered and went reluctantly after the departing men.

Letting the others go, Dusty strolled along the line of cannon. He had not sufficient men for one to each fuse and had selected the Napoleons as the pieces to be left. Lighting one length of slow-match after another, he listened for some sound that would tell him their presence had been detected by the Yankees. With every passing second, the chances of the battery being saved grew slighter.

Even if one of the artillerymen should wake up, leave the tents, come over and find a burning fuse, the affair

could still meet with success. There would be a delay while
the man doused the fuse, more as he roused the camp.
Further time would be required for the sleep-dulled Yankees to understand the danger, then search for and render
innocuous the other lengths of slow- or quick-match. Most
likely some would be overlooked, particularly those in the
battery-wagon and travelling-forge. Although Dusty believed they were too far apart for it to happen, there was
always the chance of sympathetic explosions should only
one charge touch off.

At the worst, a little damage—or even if none happened—would demoralise the battery's personnel. Certainly they would lose all their horses. Their fighting
efficiency would suffer for some time to come.

Quitting the area after lighting the last fuse, Dusty loped
swiftly after the other Texans. Bringing up the rear, Billy
Jack paused to let his commanding officer catch up with
him.

"You've cut it fine, Cap'n Dusty," the sergeant major
warned chidingly. "If one of them charges'd've gone
off——"

"They didn't," Dusty pointed out, although that thought
had occurred to him.

"Bet all them fuses've gone out," Billy Jack said as they
walked on and seemed surprised to learn that they had not.
"Anyways, I figured you'd fall down 'n' bust a leg. Was
getting set to call for volunteers to come back 'n' see."

"Thanks," Dusty grinned. "Only that kind of thing'd be
more likely to happen to you than me."

"I ain't that lucky," Billy Jack protested. "If it'd've
happened to *you,* it'd be *me*'s had to go back 'n' tell Ole
Devil and Major Hondo how come *you* went to taking such
fool chan——"

The sound of the first explosion chopped off the sergeant major's complaints. Going by its slight volume, it must have been caused by a single round detonating under the barrel of a Napoleon. However, it gave a warning that could not—must not—be ignored.

"Down!" Dusty barked, raising his voice loud and disregarding as unnecessary the need for further silence.

Dropping Genaro, the men assigned to carry him to safety joined him on the ground. Responding with equal, or even greater speed, the remainder of Dusty's party prostrated themselves on the dew-sprinkled grama grass. All offered up silent prayers, or what passed for prayers in their eyes, that the less than half a mile separating them from the battery would be sufficient for safety.

On hearing Billy Jack's signal to light the fuses, Kiowa's section had swung afork the bare backs of their selected mounts. When the first explosion sounded, the already restless horses let out startled snorts and began to bolt.

"Yeeah! Texas Light!" Kiowa screeched, slamming his heels against the flanks of his mount and using its lead rope in lieu of reins.

"Yeah! Texas Light!" echoed Vern Hassle, urging forward the horse that had been Captain Luxton's pride and joy.

Controlling the animals, they sat with the skill gained during a life-long experience in matters equine. They gathered about the fleeing horses and endeavoured to direct them to where the rest of the Company waited. Ignoring the commotion that arose behind them, they concentrated on keeping the horses bunched and held together. They needed all their ability, for the animals grew increasingly more terrified as a result of what was going on to their rear.

Following close behind the first, other explosions took

apart the silence of the night. The flat bangs caused by the single rounds were swamped beneath the deeper roars as limbers disintegrated, or drowned by triple crashes as the caissons' outer chests erupted in sympathy with the central containers' ignitions. Blasted apart by the discharge of eighty-five pounds of gunpowder, the travelling-forge sprayed nails and ruined horseshoes to the consternation of the battery's personnel as they tried to escape from their bedrolls or collapsing tents. Instead of solid shot, the battery-wagon held thirty-two rounds of shell. The half-pound burster charges added to the thirty-four cart-ridges's power and aided in the obliteration of the load.

Sudden, brilliant red flashes lit up the scene and briefly exposed the pandemonium that raged in the tent lines. Across the Arkansas River, an alarm bell boomed solemnly in Little Rock and was followed by urgent bugle calls to arouse the garrison. Members of the Confederate spy ring that operated from the town, and who had informed Dusty of the battery's arrival, heard the explosions and cut the telegraph wires leading from Buller's headquarters. That would delay news of the raid being spread to other Yankee troops.

Silence returned, or something near to it, after the final explosion. The darkness closed down again, except where an occasional small flicker of flames told that a portfire, grease-bucket, or can of paint had escaped being blown to fragments only to be reduced to ashes. Coming to their feet, the Texans stared in fascination and almost disbelief towards the havoc they had caused.

"Now that was something you don't see every day," commented Sergeant Bixby with masterly understatement.

The whole material of a field artillery battery had been completely destroyed, without loss of life to either its personnel or the raiders. It had been a remarkably well-handled affair.

"Damned if I wasn't certain-sure we'd all get blowed up, being so close," Billy Jack wailed and, in further expression of his delight, continued, "I dropped onto a rock 'n' must've caved my ribs in. Likely I'll be dead from my hurts comes morning."

"Don't you die on us, that's an order!" Dusty put in. "Turn our Yankee *amigo* loose, Sergeant Bixby."

"Yo!" the noncom answered.

While his captors had been speaking, Genaro had become aware of the rapidly approaching rumble of the hoofbeats. His emotions on the matter were mingled. Owing the Texans his life, he did not wish to see them attacked, captured or killed. Yet he would like to see the destruction of his battery avenged. Then he realised that, despite their interest in the damage, the Texans must also hear the riders. Going by their lack of concern, the men about him had reason to believe that the newcomers were friends.

Set free and with the gag removed, Genaro could do little more than sit up, stifle his moans and the pain of the restored circulation to his limbs and try to work life into his aching jaws. He looked around at the riders, each leading at least one spare horse, swept to a halt before his captors' rescuers.

The Company's guidon-carrier, a tall, well-built, sandy-haired young corporal, brought a fine, large black stallion to his commanding officer. Taking the white "Jefferson Davis" campaign hat that dangled from the hilt of the sabre strapped to the low horn of his double-girthed range saddle, Dusty donned it. Genaro could see the badge on the front of the hat's crown and guessed at its shape. A silver, five-pointed star, with the letters T.L.C. across its centre set in a laurel-wreath decorated circle, being modelled on the Sovereign State of Texas' coat-of-arms. It was an insignia all too well-known to the Yankee troops in Arkansas, but Genaro still felt curious.

"Who—Who's that officer?" the artilleryman inquired of Bixby, as Dusty swung astride the stallion.

"That, sir," the sergeant answered, a ring of pride in his voice, "is Captain Dustine Edward Marsden Fog, commanding Company "C" of the Texas Light Cavalry. You can tell it to your battery's officer, if he asks."

"Sure, I'll remember," Genaro muttered; but he had no intention of passing on his information.

If he could not be found in the morning, it would be assumed that the Rebels had carried him off; or that he had been left behind and perished in the destruction of the battery's material. Either way, the means to desert in comparative safety lay open before him. After watching the Texans ride off to the west, Genaro turned and started walking in what he believed to be an easterly direction.

Ten men, led by Dusty's second-in-command, joined Kiowa's hard-pressed section and helped them bring the terrified Yankee horses under control. With exclamations of satisfaction, the sergeant's party exchanged their bare-backed borrowed mounts for the comfort and greater safety of their own saddled horses.

Slightly over six foot in height, 1st Lieutenant Charles William Henry Blaze had wide shoulders and a strongly-made frame. He was Dusty's cousin, also eighteen, and they had grown up together in the Rio Hondo country. Under his campaign hat, a fiery thatch of ever-untidy hair gave him his commonly-used sobriquet "Red" and matched the pugnacious aspect of his freckled, good-looking face. Adopting Dusty's lead in matters sartorial, his collar sported only two bars and his "chicken guts" were formed of a single strand of brain. Two walnut-handled Army Colts rode butts-forward in his holster and he drew them cavalry-fashion instead of copying Dusty's cross-hand technique.

Like his smaller cousin, Red was building a name; but it was for hot-headed, quick-tempered, reckless audacity and an almost unrivalled ability to become involved in any fight that took place in his vicinity. There had been some comment among the senior officers of the Regiment when Dusty had taken Red as his subordinate in Company "C." However, Dusty recognised one prime virtue in his cousin that older men tended to overlook. Given a job to do, Red accepted his responsibility, handled it competently, and let nothing swerve him before its completion.

Coming together with the rest of the Company about a mile from the ruined battery, Red gave his delighted congratulations to his cousin. Then Kiowa rode up to make his report.

"Couldn't hold 'em all, Cap'n Dusty," The Indian featured sergeant-scout apologised, with a respectful tone that he did not use to every officer. "We lost us a few."

Very few, Dusty concluded as he studied the riderless mass of horses. Counting six per team for each limber, caisson, the battery-wagon and the travelling-forge, with at least a dozen saddle-mounts, they had made a fine haul. Dusty was willing to bet that Kiowa's men had not lost twenty of the animals during the wild stampede through the darkness.

"You've kept plenty," the small Texan praised. "Let's go. I want some miles between us and Little Rock comes morning."

"It'd be best," Red agreed. Then as they rode at the

head of the Company's four-abreast column in the wake of the herd of captured horses, he went on, "Reckon Uncle Devil can find use for even a bunch of Yankee crow-bait, Cousin Dusty."

Red had the Texan's inborn contempt for the lack of horse-savvy shown by the majority of Yankees who opposed them.

"Likely," Dusty replied. "He'll be pleased to get them."

"Pleased enough to give us a furlough?" Red suggested, but he did not sound too hopeful.

"Maybe," Dusty grinned. "Only it's more likely he'll have something else in mind for us when we get back."

General Jackson Baines Hardin, better known as "Ole Devil," scowled at the sheet of paper in his hand. Considering that he held an official communication from an important member of the Confederate States' Government, his whole attitude was anything but polite, impressed or respectful.

There was always something sardonic, devilish even, in Ole Devil's sharp-featured, tanned face and black eyes. It told of a temperament fiery, explosive, hard-as-nails, but with the saving grace of understanding human nature and possessing a sense of humour. Tall, ramrod-straight, his lean figure was ideally set off by the uniform of a Confederate States' Army's major general. No martinet or blind disciplinarian, he was held in the greatest respect and admiration by the men who served under him.

Since assuming command of the Confederate's Army of Arkansas and North Texas, Ole Devil had halted the Yankees' formerly triumphant advance across the Toothpick State and ended the Union's hopes of invading Northern Texas. In the opinion of many expert observers, if the

South had been able to supply him with more men, arms and equipment, he might have thrown the superiorly-numbered Union forces into retreat and pushed them out of Arkansas. As it was, he held the lands west of the Ouachita and Caddo Rivers, compelling the North to retain numbers of troops on the eastern banks who might otherwise have been diverted to more profitable battle fronts.

By skillfully deploying and manipulating his limited manpower, Ole Devil not only held his ground, but struck hard, telling blows at his enemies. Under his command, he had fewer regiments than those available to his Union opposite number. However, his soldiers had a higher morale and showed a greater determination in action. That could be accounted for by the fact that they were predominantly Texans or Arkansans, fighting to protect, or regain their home States.

While Ole Devil's infantry held the banks of the Ouachita River and its tributary, the Caddo, his cavalry crossed to raid, harass or destroy the Federal Army's personnel and supplies. For the most part native Texans, his cavalrymen had been born and raised in a land where a horse was no mere means of transport, but a vital necessity to life. Taught early to handle weapons and ride, trained by fighting against Mexican *bandidos,* bad whites, or hostile Indians, his Texans were well-suited to the Napoleonic art of making war support war. The Lone Star State fed, clothed and mounted them, but they relied upon the Yankees to produce their specialised military requirements. At a conservative estimate, three-quarters of Ole Devil's command carried Union-manufactured weapons and fired Northern-made ammunition at their Federal enemies.

All in all, the Confederate States' Government had good reason to feel satisfied with Ole Devil's handling of the

Army of Arkansas and North Texas. Yet there were times
when his superiors annoyed and exasperated him. He not
only had to retain control of the west side of the boundary
rivers with little more than their moral support, but occasionally they passed to him the damnedest requests or instructions.

Coming to his feet, Ole Devil glared across the desk at
the man who had delivered the message. They were in
what had been the library of a fine old colonial-style house
on the outskirts of Prescott. Presented by its owner as a
combined headquarters for the general and the Texas Light
Cavalry, the building and especially Ole Devil's office had
been as carefully maintained as while in its owner's hands.
There was a kind of spartan comfort about the room which
suited Ole Devil's personality and particularly matched his
present mood.

"Have you read this blasted thing, Beau?" Ole Devil
demanded, waving the document angrily.

Major Beauregard Amesley could hardly have avoided
doing so. Before the War, he had been a fencing master
with a justly-renowned *salle des armes* in New Orleans. He
had been wounded early in the conflict between North and
South and left with a permanent limp that precluded further
active service. So he had accepted the post as Ole Devil's
aide-de-camp. In addition to handling the general's affairs,
Amesley also gave fencing instruction to the young officers
of the Texas Light Cavalry and they in turn occasionally
put his lessons to good use.

"I have, sir," Amesley admitted, then stood like a man
waiting for an explosion to take place.

The wait was not prolonged. Cutting loose with a furious blast of a snort, Ole Devil flung the offending paper
on to the desk.

"So I've got to release this Captain Bertram Gilbertson, of the New Hampstead Volunteers, have him escorted from Murfreesboro to the Snake Ford of the Caddo and there exchange him for Captain Charles de Malvoisin."

"You know why, sir."

"I know *why!*" Ole Devil confirmed grimly. "Young de Malvoisin had to be clever and cross the Ouachita on an unofficial raid, then got himself captured. Now we have to arrange for him to be set free. If his men hadn't escaped, I'd say to hell with him. God blast all hot-headed young French-Creoles. I should never have let him into my command."

"His father's not without influence in our Government, sir," Amesley pointed out in a placatory manner.

"Influence!" Ole Devil spat out the word as if it burned his mouth. "What the Southern States need, Beau, is more cooperation and coordination and a whole heap less *influence*. Well, damn it, I suppose we'll have to waste men and time to effect this infernal exchange."

"The order stresses the extreme urgency of making it, sir," Amesley said.

"That's probably so that young de Malvoisin can be on hand to attend his sister's birthday ball," the general sniffed. "Do you know anything about this Gilbertson, Beau? Are we getting a fair trade?"

"I'm not sure, sir," admitted Amesley. "His name doesn't mean anything to me but the New Hampstead Volunteers aren't the best outfit Buller's got. Even if he did put up most of the money to organise and equip it."

"If Gilbertson's got two legs, two arms, a pair of eyes and ears that work, the Yankees are getting the best of the deal," Ole Devil rumbled. "Who can I send to handle the exchange?"

"Gilbertson has the right to expect an officer of equal rank as his escort, sir. It's military courtesy and a convention of war."

"If that's supposed to be a comfort to me, Beau, believe me, it isn't one."

"No, sir," Amesley replied, "Company 'C' came in last night."

"I saw Dustine's report," Ole Devil answered. "It hardly seems fair to give him the chore, he did so well. Still, it ought to be straightforward enough. A furlough even, although I don't suppose he'll think of it that way." Grinning frostily, he raised his voice in a bellow. "Sergeant major! Give Captain Fog my compliments and tell him I want to see him as soon as convenient; whether it's convenient or not."

Gripping the knife so that its long blade extended below the heel of his hand, the big man rushed at Dusty Fog. Up whipped the man's right arm, then it propelled the weapon downwards in the direction of the small Texan's shoulder. Throwing up his hands, Dusty crossed his wrists and interposed them between himself and the knife.

Descending into the upper section of the X-shape formed by Dusty's arms, the man's wrist came to a halt before the knife could reach its collarbone target. Transferring his left hand rapidly to the man's right wrist, Dusty laid his thumb along the back of the knife-hand. Advancing a pace towards his attacker, Dusty curled his right arm underneath and behind the raised elbow to fold its fingers over the inside of the trapped hand. All the time, Dusty continued to move his feet. He stopped alongside and facing towards the man's rear, elevating the ensnared arm. Delivering a swift stamping kick to the back of his assailant's right knee, Dusty tumbled him to the straw-covered floor of the big barn. Immediately on feeling the other going down, Dusty released the arm to avoid injuring him.

Excited and interested comments rose from the assembled soldiers. A dozen recently enlisted recruits, they were undergoing the final stages of their training before joining the Texas Light Cavalry's Companies. The demonstration of unarmed self-defence had been put on at the request of the big, burly sergeant who sprawled at Dusty's feet.

"You all right, Ditch?" Dusty inquired.

"Sure, cap'n," the sergeant replied, rising and retrieving the blunt knife.

"That's what I figure's the best way to handle a feller using a knife Indian fashion," Dusty told the recruits, "Don't try to grab at and catch hold of the arm. If you miss it, you're dead. Cross your wrists and block his hand, then do like I did. Only do it fast——You've got something to say, soldier?"

One of the recruits was a tall, well-made youngster slightly less than Dusty's age. Handsome, black-haired, he had an air of cocky self-assurance. While the small Texan had been speaking, he muttered to his companions.

"That's *bueno* when you're facing Injuns," the recruit answered, showing no embarrassment at being singled out. "Only it wouldn't work so good happen you come up again' a greaser or somebody's knows how to handle a knife properly."

Looking the speaker over, Dusty silenced the sergeant's angry rumble. All too well Dusty knew Tracey Prince's kind. Full of notions about the extent of their own salty toughness, they frequently needed convincing that the small captain held his rank by something more than being Ole Devil Hardin's nephew. Dusty had always found that a practical demonstration worked far better than words.

"I'm not sure how you mean, soldier," Dusty said

quietly, in a tone that would have screamed warnings to any member of Company "C," "Give him the knife, sergeant. Then he can show us what it's all about."

"Yo!" answered Ditch, offering Prince the knife hilt first and eyeing the recruit in a pitying manner.

The sergeant's attitude went unnoticed by Prince. Flickering a grin at his companions, the recruit accepted the training weapon and stepped into the centre of the open space. He held the hilt so that the blade protruded ahead of his right thumb and forefinger. Crouching slightly and showing that he had picked up some skill in the use of a fighting knife, he suddenly assailed Dusty with a series of rapidly-executed slashes and jabs. None came close to connecting with the fast-moving captain. Nor, at first, did Dusty attempt to disarm his attacker. Instead he contented himself with evasive tactics, side-stepping, twisting away, ducking beneath or bounding clear of the weapon.

Hearing his companions' sniggers combined with his repeated failures infuriated Prince. Letting out an exasperated snort, he tossed the knife from his right hand and caught it in the left. Executing the exchange with smooth precision, he drove his weapon into a savage thrust directed at his unsuspecting victim's midriff.

Unfortunately for Prince, his "victim" was anything but unsuspecting.

Swinging his left foot to the rear, Dusty pivoted his torso away from the advancing blade. As the knife rushed past him, carried onwards by the impetus of Prince's lunge, Dusty whipped up his right arm. Striking beneath Prince's right forearm, Dusty forced it into the air. Then the small Texan's left hand flashed across to grip Prince's raised wrist. Bending his right elbow, Dusty removed his blocking arm and carried it in front of his chest. From there, he lashed the heel of his clenched fist into the soldier's *solar plexus*.

Breath exploded from Prince's lungs, for the blow had not been a light one. The knife clattered to the floor as he clutched at the stricken area and doubled over. Releasing the trapped wrist, Dusty caught the discomforted Prince by the scruff of the neck and gave a sharp heave. Flung bodily across the barn, the recruit landed on his hands and knees in an empty stall.

"Now I'd say that's a tolerable fair way of handling a feller who uses his knife like a greaser," Sergeant Ditch announced and the other recruits laughed.

At that moment, the regimental sergeant major arrived and delivered Ole Devils' message verbatim.

"I reckon it's convenient now," Dusty grinned, collecting his gunbelt from the wall of a stall and buckling it on. "How many of these fellers're for me, Sergeant Ditch?"

"Only three, cap'n," Ditch answered apologetically. "You don't get your old hands killed off fast enough to need more."

"I'll try to change that," Dusty promised. "If you think they're ready, have them move their gear to my Company's lines when they get through here."

"Yo!" the sergeant replied. "Trouble being, I'm not sure one of 'em's ready yet a-whiles."

Following the noncom's sardonic glance to where Prince was climbing slowly to his feet, Dusty nodded agreement. However, one did not waste time gossiping when General Ole Devil Hardin said come as soon as convenient. Collecting his hat, Dusty left the barn with the sergeant major. Prince lurched from the stall and scowled at his companions, noticing the mocking grins on their faces.

"I likes a feller's quits when he's ahead," Prince declared. "If——"

"If Cap'n Fog'd been so minded," Ditch put in coldly, his patience wearing dangerously thin, "he'd've bust your arm, or your fool neck. You've maybe seen Tommy Okasi around headquarters?"

"That Chinee runt's works for Ole Devil?" Prince replied. "Sure, I've seen him."

Going by the recruit's tone, he did not regard the sight as being worthy of interest or comment.

"Tommy allows he ain't no Chinee, but comes from some place name of Japan—wherever that be," Ditch elaborated. "No matter where he hails from, he knows some jim-dandy fighting tricks and he's taught Cap'n Dusty all of 'em."

Although the claim tended slightly toward overstatement, none of the recruits felt like challenging it. They had just seen enough to warn them that Captain Dusty Fog possessed some out-of-the-ordinary knowledge and ability when it came to bare-handed fighting.

However, Ole Devil Hardin's Oriental personal servant had not taught Dusty all his extensive repertoire of "jim-dandy fighting tricks." He had, nevertheless passed on sufficient knowledge of *jujitsu* and *karate*—all but unknown at that period in the Western Hemisphere—for Dusty to possess a decided advantage when tangling with larger, heavier men.

"Could be they ain't so all-fired 'jim-dandy' second time you go again' 'em," Prince muttered, wanting to avoid sounding impressed.

"I wouldn't know," Ditch growled. "Nobody I've met's been hawg-stupid enough to take a second whirl. Happen you feel so inclined, you'll maybe get your chance. You, Berns 'n' Svenson can tote your gear across the Company

'C's' lines as soon as you're dismissed."

"Company 'C'," repeated Prince, delighted to learn that he would soon be on active duty. Then the full significance of the words struck him. "Hey! That's——"

"Yeah," Sergeant Ditch finished for him with a malicious grin. "That's Cap'n Fog's Company."

"Pick up Gilbertson at Murfreesboro, Dustine," Ole Devil ordered, showing no sign that his favourite nephew stood at ease before his desk. "You'll not get from the camp to the Snake Ford in one day's ride with him along, so you'll have to spend the night in the hotel at Amity."

"Yes, sir," Dusty replied.

"It'll be easy enough," Ole Devil continued. "And, if I remember correctly, Frank Jex at Murfreesboro sets a good table. We must go up there—on a tour of inspection—one day soon, Beau."

"Yo!" Amesley answered, then looked at the small Texan. "Remember, Dusty, if Gilbertson can escape before you reach the Snake Ford, the exchange can't be put into effect."

"I understand, sir," Dusty replied.

"What escort will you be taking?" Ole Devil inquired.

"A sergeant, four men. That ought to do it, sir. I'll not need a large party."

"That'll be enough, I shouldn't think Gilbertson will bother about trying to escape. How about the rest of your wild men while you're away?"

"I'll leave Cous—Mr. Blaze enough work to keep them occupied, sir."

"See you do," Ole Devil warned. "I don't want them rampaging around Prescott. It'd be enough to turn the local citizens into Yankees."

Already, with pride in their solid achievements behind

them, Company "C" regarded themselves as the elite of the best damned fighting cavalry regiment in the whole Confederate States' Army. As was always the case, they insisted that their company commander was the sole authority to which they should be accountable and considered that few other officers had the right to give them orders.

While Ole Devil recognised the military value of such a spirit, especially in the kind of war circumstances compelled him to fight, he wished to avoid friction within his command or among the local citizens. So he wanted to be sure that Company "C's" more reckless members were held in check. Dusty could do it, but Ole Devil wondered if Red Blaze possessed the type of personality to do so. Knowing his cousin, Dusty felt no such doubts as long as he took certain precautions before leaving.

"I'll have a few words with them before I go, sir," Dusty promised. "Will that be all, sir?"

"It will," Ole Devil confirmed. "Get him there and effect the exchange, Dustine. Bring de Malvoisin back here with you. You're dismissed."

Saluting, Dusty made an about-face and marched from the office. Leaving the building, he made his way in the direction of his Company's lines. Strolling along, he gave thought to the composition of the escort. There could be only one choice for his second-in-command. Red would need help to control the Company's high spirits. It could best be supplied by Billy Jack with the able backing of Sergeants Bixby and "Stormy" Weather. While Kiowa Cotton also held rank as sergeant, his duties were riding scout and he had small interest in disciplinary or administrative matters. Conditions might arise during the delivery of the Yankee prisoner where Kiowa's specialised talents would be invaluable. For the rest, Dusty would select the men least likely to provoke the kind of incident that Ole Devil wished to avoid.

Hearing his name called, Dusty came out of his reverie and saw Ditch approaching. The sergeant saluted and said, "I've sent your recruits over, Cap'n Dusty. Berns, Svenson —and Prince."

"I know Phil Berns and Ollie Svenson from back home," Dusty replied. "What's this Prince yahoo like, Ditch?"

"Good with a gun. Better'n fair with a hoss."

"Now get to the things he's not so 'good' or 'better than fair' at."

"He's a mite uppy, like you saw. Which he'll maybe need his toes taking up a couple of times afore he shapes up. That's why I assigned him to *your* Company."

"Thanks." Dusty said dryly, but he was pleased with the implied compliment.

A long-serving career-soldier, Ditch knew men and could figure out how best to handle them. So he had decided that Dusty was the officer best suited to tame Prince and turn the recruit into a useful soldier.

If a horse on a roundup insisted on repeatedly breaking out of the wranglers' rope-corral,* the boss would tell his best roper to "take its toes up" on the next departure. By tossing his loop around the recalcitrant horse's forefeet, the roper would slam it to the ground with sufficient force to knock better sense into it, or break its neck. If the latter happened, the rancher would regard it as small enough price for preventing the bad habit spreading among the rest of the *remuda*.

---

* The use of a rope-corral is described in *Trail Boss*.

Such drastic treatment would not be applied to Prince, but he might require a sharp, painful lesson before he accepted discipline.

Continuing his interrupted journey, Dusty approached his company's lines of cone-shaped Sibley tents. He discovered Billy Jack making the three recruits welcome before assigning them to their quarters. Standing with his back to Dusty, the gangling sergeant major was obviously unaware of his commanding officer's arrival.

"Cap'n Dusty don't make favourites," Billy Jack was saying. "He's just naturally mean to everybody. So you-all keep one thing in mind. In this outfit, there's two ways of going on. How the captain wants it and the *wrong* way. Do your work and life'll go so easy you'll reckon you'd been born rich. Make fuss and you'll wish you'd never been born at all."

"I couldn't have put it better, sergeant major," Dusty declared.

Calling the recruits to attention, Billy Jack performed a much smarter than usual about-face and saluted. Dusty returned the compliment, then turned his grey eyes to the trio. Glancing briefly at Berns and Svenson, he let his gaze stay longer on Prince's face. Then he dropped his eyes to the gunbelt with its holsters tied low on the recruit's thighs. Prince had the kind of attitude best calculated to raise Red Blaze's ire. Until the youngster had learned to accept discipline, he would be better away from Dusty's fiery-tempered cousin. However, Dusty wanted to avoid making the matter too obvious.

"Get your gear settled in," the small Texan ordered. "Inspect their horses, sergeant major. I'll be taking Svenson and Prince with me on patrol in the morning."

"Yo!" Billy Jack replied, looking more apprehensive than interested. "Where're we headed this time?"

"You and the Company'll be headed over to Captain Streeton's cannon battery," Dusty replied. "I want you to know all about handling them by the time I get back."

"Back?"

"I've got to collect a Yankee prisoner from Murfrees-boro and take him for exchange on the Snake Ford of Caddo."

"I didn't reckon Yankee prisoners was worth anything in trading," Billy Jack sniffed and nodded towards Prince and the stocky, blond-haired Svenson. "Will you be wanting somebody beside them?"

"Sure," Dusty replied. "I'll take Kiowa and Graveling; and I'd best have Surtees along. Rations for a week, fifty rounds a man for their revolvers, twenty for their saddle-guns."

"Does Surtees need his bugle?"

"He's paid for blowing it, so have him bring it along. I don't want to have to ask the Arkansas Rifles for the loan of a bugler, they might think we don't have any in the Texas Light."

Fully aware of the rivalry which existed between the Arkansas Rifles, an infantry regiment, and his outfit, Billy Jack understood Dusty's point.

"They'd likely put it around we use smoke-signals if you did," the lanky sergeant major admitted. "I'll warn Kiowa and the fellers."

"Bueno!" Dusty answered. "We'll be pulling out an hour after reveille in the morning."

"They'll be ready," Billy Jack assured him.

"Huh!" snorted Prince, after Dusty had walked away. "I didn't join the Army to be nursemaid to a Yankee pris-oner."

"Happen you don't like it, go tell Cap'n Dusty you ain't going," Billy Jack advised coldly. "Only don't do it while

I'm around. I hates to see the sight of *privates'* blood getting spilled."

"You sure it'd be the *private's* blood?" Prince asked.

"So sure that, happen you're *loco* enough to do it, I'll go start writing to tell your folks how you died," the sergeant major replied. "Go put up your gear. Feller's tough as you'll be a great help to the cooks."

"Huh?" grunted the Prince.

"You got so much *brio escondido** that you can work some of it off peeling potatoes for 'em," Billy Jack explained. "Get moving."

For all his mournful, hang-dog aspect and fake-miserable temperament, the sergeant major was a shrewd judge of character. Unless he missed his guess, young Tracey Prince would either change his ways in the near future or receive a well-deserved lesson in manners. If Prince clashed wills with Dusty Fog, Billy Jack had no doubts as to what the result will be.

Always a realist, Ole Devil Hardin had grown increasingly doubtful that the South could win the War. His decision to support the Confederate States had not been motivated by a desire for the right to possess slaves; for he owned none and had no wish to do so. In fact, despite its use by Northern propagandists as a means of justifying and ennobling their cause, the Slavery issue had not been the sole reason for the secession.

Far more important, to most Texans' way of thinking, had been an infringement of the right of each, or any State —as a sovereign government—to secede from the Union if its affairs and interests became incompatible with those of the Federal Congress.

* Brio escondido: hidden vigour, stamina of a high order.

Since becoming a part of the Union, Texas had been shabbily treated. Having disbanded its efficient Ranger battalions, the State had repeatedly been refused the military protection promised by the Federal government. So the majority of Texans had become disenchanted with the Northern States. On top of that, many Texans had close family ties in the other seceding States. So the Lone Star State had voted by a two-thirds majority to join the Confederate States and Ole Devil had offered his clan's services.

Slowly but surely, the North's industrial and economic superiority was crushing the South. Courage and prowess on the battlefield could not avail in the long run. Even without his own humanitarian feelings and sense of chivalry, that factor had made Ole Devil determined that his prisoner-of-war camps would not follow the lead of Andersonville and other Confederate establishments.

To be fair to the staffs of the other Southern camps, much of the terrible conditions, the shortages of food, clothing and medical supplies, could be blamed upon the Yankees themselves. The United States Navy's blockade of Southern ports had restricted the import of many vital commodities and, not unnaturally, the Confederate authorities had given priority to their own people rather than to their captured enemies.

So there were mitigating circumstances for the adverse conditions in the majority of Confederate camps. Far more so than in those commanded by the Union's intellectual General Smethurst.* There, starvation, ill-treatment and cruelty were permitted, encouraged even, by Smethurst and his kind out of vicious malice against men who had

---

* More of General Smethurst's story can be read in *Back to the Bloody Border* and in *The Hooded Riders*.

refused to give blind acquiescence to their "liberal" beliefs.

Knowing that men who received reasonable treatment would remember it in later years, Ole Devil had made arrangements and issued strict instructions concerning the prisoners-of-war taken by his command.

Caution demanded that the Yankee officers and men be kept separate; as did military tradition. So there were two camps, perched on the tops of hills about a mile apart, not far from Murfreesboro, seat of Pike County. Inside the stout log pallisades, the enlisted men occupied tents and the officers were quartered in wooden cabins.

Many of the enlisted men fed better than any other time in their lives, for Texas longhorns were such a cheap and easily obtainable commodity that they received beef at least once a day. Such had been the success of Ole Devil's system that there had never been an attempt to escape from Murfreesboro. In fact, there had been considerable reluctance to accept on the part of several enlisted men who had been offered their freedom and the chance to return to their respective regiments east of the Ouachita.

Wanting to get his assignment over as quickly as possible, Dusty had sent Kiowa on ahead of the rest of the escort. Riding a two-horse relay, the Indian-dark sergeant had reached the camp the previous night and informed its commanding officer that the exchange was due to be implemented.

At ten o'clock on the second day after receiving his orders from the Ole Devil, Dusty sat in the office of the camps' commanding officer and watched Colonel Jex read his authorisation to collect Captain Gilbertson. White-haired, elderly, with a pleasant face, Jex had been a cavalry officer all his service before coming to the more sedentary occupation of running the prisoner-of-war camps. Looking at Dusty as he laid down the paper, Jex expressed the amiability and comradeship that stemmed from their mutual membership of the mounted arm of the service.

"If Gilbertson wasn't the son of the top soft-shell politician in New Hampstead," Jex remarked after the conventional greetings had ended, "I'd wonder why the hell Buller wanted him back. I've got career-officers here who'd be far greater use to the North."

"What kind of man is he?" Dusty inquired.

"If he was a horse, I wouldn't use him to breed mules," Jex sniffed, then cocked his head and listened to the footsteps crossing the porch to his office door. "This'll be him now."

Turning, Dusty watched the door open and Captain Gilbertson walk in. Clad in an untidy uniform, the man for exchange proved to be tall, thick-set, with heavy, sullen features. Cold, suspicious eyes darted from Jex to Dusty and roamed over the small Texan's figure with an almost insulting gaze. Slouching across to the colonel's desk, the Yankee Volunteer threw up a grudging salute.

"Captain Fog, this is Captain Gilbertson, New Hampstead Volunteers," Jex introduced, struggling to sound polite. "Captain Gilbertson, may I present your escort? This is Captain Fog of the Texas Light Cavalry."

Again the cold eyes turned Dusty's way. There was a hint of condescension in Gilbertson's attitude. He acknowledged the introduction with only the slightest inclination of his head. Although willing to be friendly, Dusty kept his right hand at his side and made no greater gesture in reply than he had been given.

"If it's convenient to you, captain," Dusty said evenly, "I'd like to leave just after noon."

"I'm ready to go straight away," Gilbertson answered, his voice well-educated, arrogant and anything but polite. "How soon can we start?"

The ungracious response drew an angry intake of breath from Jex. Up to that moment, the colonel had been intending to ask the two young captains to be his guests for lunch. Faced with such blatant bad manners, Jex felt disinclined to offer his hospitality to the Yankee.

"You can leave when you're ready, Captain Fog," the colonel said blandly, without looking at Gilbertson. "I hope that you'll have an uneventful journey, and that you will call by to dine with me on your return."

"It will be my pleasure, sir," Dusty replied. "With your permission, we'll make a start."

Walking over to the cupboard at the left of his desk, Jex opened it and took out a Union Army weapon belt with a sabre on its slings. Bringing them across to Gilbertson, he held them out.

"Your sword, captain."

Jerking his eyes from their scrutiny of Dusty, Gilbertson looked at the weapon with an air of mistrust. He seemed puzzled and surprised by Jex's action, maybe even wondering if its return might be some kind of trick. Without a word of thanks, he accepted and buckled on the belt.

"Have you all your other property, captain?" Dusty asked.

"All your men le——" Gilbertson began, then shrugged. "I've got it all."

"May we go, sir?" Dusty went on to Jex.

"You're dismissed," the colonel confirmed.

With a more sociable prisoner, the colonel would have said more. A glance at Dusty assured Jex that his motives and brusque tone were understood. Saluting, the small Texan and the Volunteer turned and left the office. Curious officer-prisoners watched as the two captains walked from the administration compound and crossed to the main gates. Listening to the ribald comments directed at Gilbertson, Dusty concluded that his unpopularity extended to his companions in the camp. Certainly none of them displayed displeasure, or regret, at seeing him leave.

Kiowa and the four privates waited outside the pallisade. Joining his men and accepting his stallion's reins from the bugler, Dusty indicated the second of the horses held by Svenson.

"Will you use that one, captain?" Dusty asked.

Looking at the horse, Gilbertson gave a sniff. It had the appearance of being easy-going, but did not approach the superb quality of the animals to be used by his escort. While its gentle disposition and sober temperament would make it a pleasant animal to ride, it could not hope to outrun the Texans' mounts. Despite the way in which the words had been framed, the Volunteer knew that he had no choice but accept.

"It'll do," Gilbertson growled.

Considering that he was being released from captivity and returned to his own people, Gilbertson showed little change in his sullen attitude. With a surly scowl, he swung astride his borrowed horse. Watching his escort mount, he reached conclusions about them. That third bar on the captain's collar had not been in place for long. For one so young to have reached such a rank hinted that family connections rather than outstanding achievements had taken him there. Apart from the sergeant, the rest of the escort had the appearance of youth, inexperience even. That sergeant would be a decisive element in the event of trouble. Hard-faced and dangerous, he would not be a man amenable to discipline and might require watching.

On the move, Dusty told Kiowa to range ahead, then sent Graveling and Surtees out on the flanks. Watching them go, Gilbertson revised his opinion. For all their smart appearance and new-looking uniforms, those two had seen service. The Volunteer did not need to ask why Dusty was taking such precautions.

After a few attempts had failed during the early days of Ole Devil Hardin assuming defensive positions west of the Ouachita and Caddo Rivers, the Yankee cavalry had shown little tendency to cross and raid. Clearly Captain Fog did not believe in taking chances. There were other factors to be considered besides official Union Army action. Thinking of them, Gilbertson almost approved of his escort's precautions.

Guerillas, for the most part little better than marauding bands of thieves, roamed both sides of the rivers. Under the pretence of fighting for the North or the South, they looted, pillaged and committed outrages. They would not hesitate to snatch up a Yankee officer, or a Rebel for that matter so that he could be ransomed by his friends or brought by his enemies. Misguided Southern patriots formed a smaller, but no less real threat. One of them might decide to shoot a Yankee soldier out of malice and without thought of how his actions might affect his own Army. Gilbertson was pleased that his escort seemed aware of the dangers.

Despite all Dusty's precautions, or possibly because of them, the day's journey went by uneventfully. They had ridden at a steady pace, held down to the limit of the slowest horse. At first Dusty had tried to open a conversation, but Gilbertson displayed such a reluctance to reply that the attempts ended. Yet the Volunteer's attitude puzzled Dusty. Other Union officers with whom the small Texan had come in contact had talked, joked even. What Dusty failed to take into consideration was that they had been professional soldiers, men who fought as their duty and responded to the friendship of chivalrous enemies who followed the conventions of war.

Towards sundown, the party crossed the boundary between Pike and Clark Counties and entered the small town of Amity. The arrival of a Union officer, even though accompanied by a Confederate captain and five enlisted men from the Texas Light Cavalry, attracted considerable attention. Women and children came from the houses to follow the riders. Discarding their traditional pastimes of pitching horseshoes at the back of the livery barn, or hard-wintering* on the porch of the general store, elderly and middle-aged men converged on the newcomers. Dusty noticed that Gilbertson looked uneasy, nervous almost, and darted worried glances at the civilians.

Nothing untoward happened and Dusty's party turned their horses toward the front of the small hotel. Glancing up, Dusty saw an unshaven face at the window of a first floor room. It withdrew on finding itself observed. Then the people attracted the small Texan's attention.

"Where'd you get him, Cap'n?" asked an old man sporting the badge of town constable, but not wearing a gun.

"Why's he still wearing that toad-sticker?" another of the crowd demanded, indicating Gilbertson's sabre.

Dusty was saved from answering the questions by the crowd pressing closer. Letting out a snort, his huge black stallion cut loose with both iron shod rear hooves and caused a rapid movement away from it. Quitting his saddle, he quietened his mount down and looked over his shoulder.

---

* Hard-wintering: gossiping or story-telling, from the old men's habit of discussing the severity of the winters in their younger days.

"Keep back please, folks," Dusty requested.

"You come crowding in too close behind any of these hosses, and you're likely to wind up picking shoeing-iron out of your teeth," Kiowa elaborated, dropping to the ground and facing the crowd. "Hold back there, all of you."

"Haul back, folks," the constable continued, conscious of his official status. "Come on, give these Texas gents room to move."

"*Gracias* marshal," Dusty drawled as the people obeyed.

"Ain't got no jail-house, 'cepting for the root-cellar at my place, cap'n," the constable said respectfully. "You can put him in that, happen you want to."

"Damn it, F—Captain Fog!" Gilbertson barked. "I'm an officer——"

"It's all right, marshal," Dusty put in, ignoring the outburst. "I'll tend to him. Will you show my men to the livery barn, please?"

"Sure will, cap'n," the constable agreed.

"Kiowa, take Prince, Graveling and Svenson with you," Dusty ordered. "Tend to the horses and leave Prince on guard while you come to bed down and eat."

"Yo!" Kiowa replied, taking the reins of Dusty's stallion. "Let's go."

Accompanied by the constable, Kiowa's party led the horses away. Without satisfying the crowd's curiosity, Dusty and Gilbertson entered the hotel, followed by Surtees. The Volunteer studied Surtees again. While a bugle was suspended from the soldier's left shoulder, the Dance Bros. Army revolver in his open-topped holster had seen much use. There was a tough, capable air about the bugler that warned Gilbertson of his ability in combatant duties.

So the Yankee shelved until later certain thoughts which had run through his head on seeing the majority of his escort sent away.

Like most such establishments in small towns, the Amity Hotel did double duty as a saloon. Its front door opened into a large combined dining and bar-room, the counter also serving as a reception desk. At each end of the bar, a flight of stairs ascended to the first floor.

Crossing the room, Dusty gave thought to a problem. He looked at Gilbertson for a moment as they stood at the reception desk end of the counter and reached a decision.

"Captain Gilbertson," Dusty said formally. "We'll be at the Snake Ford by noon tomorrow——"

"That's so," the Volunteer agreed, acting more amiably than previously.

"Will you give me your word not to escape, or try to, between now and sun-up tomorrow?" Dusty requested. "It'll make things a heap easier for all of us."

"Of course I will," Gilbertson agreed without hesitation.

Despite the increasing determination and bitterness that had developed with each succeeding year of the War, the traditional chivalries and conventions were still generally observed. Captured officers in most cases received the privileges of their rank, especially those taken by the Army of Arkansas and North Texas. If an officer gave his parole, he would be allowed a measure of freedom and was expected to keep within the bounds of his agreement.

"Your word of honour, sir?" Dusty insisted, wanting no misunderstandings.

"My word of honour, Captain Fog," Gilbertson confirmed solemnly.

Something in the Yankee's manner disturbed Dusty, but he could not put his finger on what it might be. An officer in the Union Army's word was his bond, as binding as if he had signed the most carefully written legal agreement. Yet Dusty felt vaguely uneasy.

There appeared to be no valid reason for Gilbertson to refuse his parole. By noon the following day, at the latest, he could cross the Snake Ford of the Caddo and be free. So Dusty could see no reason why the Volunteer would want to take the risk of attempting to escape. Having pledged his word of honour, Gilbertson would not require guarding and the whole sense of tension that filled the members of the escort could disperse.

Hearing the door behind the bar open, Dusty turned his attention to it. The owner of the hotel, a short, unshaven man in old, but clean, town clothes, came to the counter. Dusty decided that he was the man who had looked down from the first floor room on their arrival.

On listening to Dusty's request for accommodation, the owner threw a scowling glare at Gilbertson. For a moment the man seemed to be on the verge of refusing. Then his eyes went to Dusty's collar and he recognised the meaning of the three bars it carried. There was an air of quiet, determined authority about the small Texan only rarely seen in one so young. More than that, the Captain wore a gun-belt with the ease of long practice. He also had the backing of a tough, salty-looking soldier; with more of them close at hand should the need for their assistance arise.

"Got me two single-bed rooms and a big 'n' is all cap'n," the owner said.

"Captain Gilbertson and I'll have the singles," Dusty decided. "Can you put my men in the other?"

"Ain't but the one bed, but I'll set mattresses on the floor for the others," the man offered.

"You've got other folks staying here?" Dusty inquired.

"A gambling man and three other fellers, cap'n. They're

just passing through. You want to see them rooms now?"

"We might as well," Dusty decided.

Going up the right hand flight of stairs, the owner turned along a narrow passage. Opening doors, he showed his vacant quarters to the soldiers. The two single rooms flanked the larger. While small, they had clean-looking beds and appeared to be comfortable enough.

"They do?" the owner asked grudgingly.

"They'll do," confirmed Dusty. "Which one do you want, captain?"

"I'll take this," Gilbertson answered, nodding to the door nearest to the head of the stairs.

If the Volunteer had refused to give his parole, Dusty would not have accepted the selection. With Gilbertson's word of honour accepted, he could choose either of the rooms.

"It's yours," Dusty said. "I hope you'll be my guest for supper tonight. And it might be best if you didn't leave the hotel unless one of us is with you."

"Damn it, I've given you my word——!" Gilbertson blazed.

"And I've accepted it. But the folks in Amity aren't used to seeing Union officers around. If somebody should see you out alone, they might figure you're trying to escape. There's no sense in taking chances, is there?"

"I suppose not. And I'll do what you suggest."

Once it had been explained, Gilbertson could see the wisdom of Dusty's suggestion and so had accepted it. In Murfreesboro, the citizens knew the meaning of a parole and had grown accustomed to seeing unescorted Yankee officers on the streets. People in a hamlet like Amity would not understand such matters.

A man stepped from a room across the passage. Dressed in dirty range-clothes, carrying an Army Colt tied low on his right thigh, he had a hard, unshaven face. Of medium height, he was clearly within the military age limits. His eyes went first to Gilbertson, then turned in Dusty's direction. Stepping from his room, he went along the passage with a pronounced limp to his left leg. That might account for why he did not wear a uniform.

"If you-all want anything, cap'n, just holler for it," the owner remarked. "Supper'll not be ready for two hours, 'less you want it sooner."

"That'll be soon enough," Dusty replied.

Going to his room, Dusty looked along the passage. The civilian was on the point of entering a door next to the second flight of stairs and stared back over his shoulder. Finding himself under observation, the man jerked his eyes to the front and disappeared through the doorway. Dusty realised that the man occupied, or had left, one of the rooms at the front of the building. Possibly it had been him and not the owner who had attracted Dusty's attention earlier.

Two and one-half hours after their arrival, Dusty accompanied Gilbertson into the barroom. Waving Kiowa and the three privates to remain seated, Dusty strolled across to a small table by the window. Looking out, he saw half-a-dozen saddled horses standing at the hotel's hitching-rail. Possibly they belonged to the lame civilian and the other two gun-hung hard-cases who stood drinking at the counter.

None of the trio turned or showed the slightest interest in the new arrivals, a thing Dusty noticed and pondered upon. Before the small Texan could reach any conclusions, the owner's wife appeared and placed plates of steaming stew before the two officers.

"Ain't got nothing else, cap'n," the woman declared,

directing her words to Dusty. "I hope it'll do."

"It'll do right well, ma'am," Dusty assured her and nodded towards the bar. "Who're those fellers?"

"Reckon they've been helping Colonel Early drive in cattle from Texas," the woman answered. "Smell like they might've been, too."

"Bad as that, huh?" Dusty grinned.

"Sure is," agreed the woman and walked away.

With so many able-bodied men serving the South, Colonel Jubal Early of the Confederate States Army's Quartermaster's Corps had to make use of whatever help he could find to deliver herds of cattle. Possibly the men had been paid off from a drive and had decided to stay in Amity for a few days on their way back to Texas. There was nothing strange, or suspicious about them being in the town; except for their too-obvious lack of interest in Dusty and the Yankee captain.

Despite giving his parole not to escape, Gilbertson showed no signs of mellowing during the meal. Having already discovered that the other had no wish for conversation, Dusty made no great effort to stimulate one. Instead he settled down to eat the tasty stew and studied his surroundings. Dusty decided that he would not be sorry to part company with the surly Yankee officer, but refused to let the Volunteer spoil his enjoyment of the meal.

When the men had finished eating, Kiowa rose and slouched across the room to the officers' table.

"Got the hosses bedded down with no fuss, Cap'n Dusty," the scout reported. "Now me 'n' the boys've fed, I'll send Graveling down to relieve young Prince so's he can come and eat."

"What do you know about those three *hombres* at the bar, Kiowa?" Dusty asked.

"Tallest name's Abe, the one with the limp's Will, 'n'

t'other's called Harpe. Allow to've been working for Jubal Early."

"Have they?"

"Could be. He takes on some hard hands. Only they don't talk Texan. East Arkansan maybe, or even Mississip', but not Texan."

"There're no ropes on those saddles," Dusty remarked, nodding towards the window. "I reckon we'll have two men on guard at the barn tonight."

"Yo!" Kiowa agreed. "I'll take Graveling and Surtees for the first trick. Then I'll sleep down there 'n' can watch the other two while they're doing their spell—Unless you want me here."

"Stop at the barn," Dusty confirmed.

Kiowa's eyes flickered briefly in Gilbertson's direction. Then the sergeant gave a barely perceptible nod of understanding. Clearly the Yankee had given his parole not to escape. In which case, Cap'n Dusty would not need to keep a strict watch over him. A bunch of excellent-quality horses would make a tempting target should the three hardcases be other than they stated. So the sensible thing was to establish a strong guard over the animals.

Swinging on his heel, Kiowa returned to the other enlisted men. After his companions had left, Svenson rose and went across to the bar. Grinning amiably, the civilian called Will told the hotel's owner—now acting as bartender—to give the soldier a drink. Before accepting, Svenson warned the trio that he was in no financial condition to return the hospitality. Waving aside the comment as of no importance, Will limped along the counter and started a conversation.

Watching the men, Dusty saw nothing unusual in Will's actions. In times of war and danger, civilians tended to forget their antipathy toward soldiers and not infrequently entertained them. Going by the gestures which were made, Will was asking Svenson why the other Texans had left and the soldier satisfied his curiosity. Then Will slapped his pockets and let out an annoyed grunt.

"Damned if I didn't leave my money upstairs," the man announced. "I'll have to go and fetch it."

Everything seemed harmless as Will went to the right side set of stairs. Yet Dusty experienced a growing sense of uneasiness as he watched the man depart. The small Texan wondered what kind of injury had caused Will's pronounced limp. It must have been of a most peculiar nature, for its effects appeared to change from leg to leg. Dragging his *right* foot awkwardly, Will disappeared up the stairs.

With a more sociable companion, even an enemy, Dusty would have mentioned and discussed the phenomenon. Deciding against trying to communicate with the surly Volunteer, the small Texan still thought about Will's disability.

Why should the man fake a limp if he worked for Jubal Early?

There seemed to be no need for such subterfuge. Bringing in cattle to help feed the fighting soldiers could be classed as a useful occupation. It would excuse a man for not being in uniform. Of course, soldiers suffering the dangers and hardships of war might be unsympathetic and not so understanding towards healthy civilians. Especially if the same civilians were employed in work that brought them wages far beyond the soldier's meagre pay.

Will might be faking an injury to avoid trouble of that kind; although he did not strike Dusty as the type of man who would go to such lengths to do so.

A deserter might adopt a limp, so as to evade being questioned and to excuse him not being in uniform. Which

did not explain Will's obvious interest in Gilbertson upstairs. Unless he had deserted from the *Union* Army and
was afraid that the Volunteer might recognise, denounce
and cause his return. That could be. There had been cases
during the war of officers, plagued by desertion among
their own men, returning captured enemy deserters. Doing
so warned their malcontents that no safe refuge awaited
them on the other side.

Recently, however, there had been a growing tendency
among the Northern and Rebel Armies to attempt to en-
courage desertion from their enemy's forces. Offers of
good treatment, safe conduct, assistance even, had been
made in the hope of seducing men from the opposition.
Perhaps Will had not heard of the change in policy, or
disbelieved it and aimed to take no chances.

Footsteps sounded on the left-side stairs; a firm, even,
heavy tread different in timbre from Will's hesitant gait.
Glancing across the room, Dusty saw that the other two
hard-cases had joined Svenson. Abe stood to the recruit's
right and Harpe lounged negligently to his left. A snort and
movement outside the building drew Dusty's attention to
the horses. Suddenly he became aware of a significant
point that had escaped his notice earlier. Instead of being
tied to the hitching-rail, the horses' reins merely dangled
across it. While such a method held trained mounts as effectively as tying them, the necessary training took time
and patience. Any man who made the effort had a good
reason for doing it. Outlaws, needing to have the means for
a fast escape, used it.

From the horses, Dusty swung his eyes in the direction
of the left side set of stairs. He studied the man who was
coming down. Dressed in a low-crowned, wide-brimmed
black hat, grey broadcloth jacket, fancy vest, frilly-
bosomed shirt, string bow-tie, slim-legged white trousers

and town boots, he had the appearance of a riverboat gambler. Clean-shaven, swarthily-handsome, he appeared to have nothing in common with the bristle-stubbled hardcases at the bar.

Yet he *did* belong to Will's party!

Dusty discovered the fact just an instant too late.

Stepping into the barroom, his right hand concealed behind his back, the newcomer did not look at the men by the counter. Although no visible signal passed between them, Abe and Harpe reacted swiftly to the gambler's arrival. Sliding his Army Colt from its holster, Abe rammed its barrel against Svenson's side. Just as rapidly, Harpe produced his Remington Army revolver and threw down on the startled hotelkeeper.

About to rise, left hand moving across in the direction of the right side Colt's butt, Dusty saw the gambler swing to face him. While turning, the man brought his right hand from behind his back. In it, he held a Starr Army revolver which he lined at the small Texan.

"Sit still, sonny!" the gambler ordered. "No heroics, unless you want to get your man and our host killed."

"Do what you want, Cap'n Dus——!" Svenson began, standing like a statue with a whiskey-filled glass halfway to his lips.

"Monte ain't fooling, soldier-boy," Abe warned, gouging the Colt's muzzle harder into Svenson's ribs.

"I'm not," the gambler assured Dusty. "My companions are men of hasty temper and with small regard for human life. You don't want two deaths on your conscience, do you, captain?"

Put that way, Dusty knew that he must restrain his intentions. If his life only had been at stake, he would have taken his chances. On producing the Starr, Monte had come to a halt and was waiting until his men had the situation under control before moving closer. So Dusty would have staked his gun-skill against the trio's across the width of the barroom. He could not if doing it would cause the deaths of two men.

"What's the idea, *hombre?*" Dusty asked and continued to rise, keeping his empty hands in plain view.

"We gentlemen of Monte Beaufort's Private Company are going to save you some time and effort, captain," the gambler replied, walking towards the two officers. "If we take your blue-clad friend off your hands, you won't need to ride all the way to Murfreesboro with him and can go back to your regiment."

"And what'll you do with him?" Dusty inquired, moving slowly around the table as he spoke.

The mention of Monte Beaufort's Private Company had already supplied the answer. To add a kind of spurious legality to their efforts, most bands of guerillas adopted military-sounding titles. Clearly the men at the hotel belonged to such an organisation. Most probably, the gambler was "Monte Beaufort."

"I reckon he'll be worth something to somebody," the gambler answered, darting a glance at the seated Yankee Volunteer. "If not——Well, it's the duty of all loyal Southerners to kill Abolitionists."

That was just about what Dusty had expected to lie behind the the men's actions. Advancing a couple of strides, Dusty stopped between his prisoner and the approaching guerilla-leader.

"Captain Gilbertson's in my care, *hombre!*" Dusty stated flatly.

"I've no quarrel with you, soldier-boy," Monte warned. "But if you don't step aside, I'll blow a hole through you."

"Pull that trigger and you're done for," Dusty replied. "If the rest of my men don't get you, Uncle Devil'll not let anybody rest until you've been hunted down and hung from a tree."

"*Uncle* Devil?" Monte growled and his two companions looked around.

"Ole Devil Hardin's my uncle," Dusty announced in a carrying voice. "My name is Dusty Fog."

By trade and natural aptitude, Monte was a fast thinker. So he considered Dusty's words and digested their implications. For one so young and insignificant to hold captain's rank hinted at important family connections. According to rumour, the Fogs shared with the Hardins and Blazes in the ownership of Texas' vast Rio Hondo County. So the small blond was most likely speaking the truth.

Having worked on Mississippi riverboats, Monte knew all about the strong inter-family loyalties possessed by Southern gentlemen. So he was aware that the short-grown captain had been correct about how Ole Devil Hardin would react to the news of his nephew's murder.

On the other hand, the commanding general of the Army of Arkansas and North Texas might be willing to overlook the abduction of the prisoner if his loss could mean damage to a favourite, kinsman's career.

By the time he had formulated his opinion and come to a decision on it, the gambler had almost reached Dusty. Giving a shrug and acting as if he had reconsidered, Monte let his revolver's barrel sag towards the floor and he made as if to turn away.

"All right," the gambler said, in tones of mock-resignation. "No shooting!"

With that, Monte rapidly reversed his direction and whipped his revolver around. Instead of burning powder, he intended to smash the barrel against the side of the small Texan's head.

Suddenly Dusty no longer looked small. In some

strange manner, he appeared to have taken on size and heft until he conveyed the impression of at least equalling Monte's height.

Far from being fooled by the gambler's apparent change of heart, Dusty had expected some such reaction. Instead of trying to draw back, or dodge under the blow, Dusty stepped within its arc. Up rose his hands in the kind of X-block he had used against Sergeant Ditch's knife attack, but he did not intend to restrict himself to his former comparatively mild protective measures while disarming his present assailant.

As Monte's wrist impacted into the side of the "X" and halted, Dusty continued to move with devastating speed. Breaking open his block the instant it had served its purpose, Dusty caught Monte's wrist from below with his left hand and turned the gun-filled fist palm upwards. Bending his right elbow, Dusty closed his other fingers over the top of the gambler's bicep. At the same time, Dusty pivoted to the left so that he halted with his back to Monte's belly.

Snapping down with his hands, Dusty slammed the back of Monte's trapped elbow onto the left shoulder of his tunic. Doing so exerted a dangerous pressure against the joint and came close to breaking it. With a yelp, Monte released his hold on the Starr and it fell at Gilbertson's feet. Nor had the gambler's troubles ended. Sinking to his left knee, Dusty catapulted his larger, heavier assailant over his shoulder. Smashing into the wall with his rump, Monte crumpled onto the top of the table at which the officers had eaten their meal and sprawled limply across it.

Having known Dusty since childhood in Polveroso City, Svenson had not been misled by the small Texan's passive behaviour. So the recruit had stood quietly, but ready and waiting to take full advantage of Dusty's response to the threat when it came.

Attracted by the conversation between Dusty and Monte, the two hard-cases at the bar had allowed their attention to be diverted from the men they were supposed to be guarding. On seeing how Dusty handled the gambler, Abe and Harpe hastily began to turn their weapons in his direction. They were confused by the sudden and—as it appeared to them—miraculous turn of events. Nor did the stocky blond recruit give them time to recover from the shock of seeing the diminutive captain almost casually flip the much heftier Monte over his shoulder.

Jerking his wrist to the right, Svenson propelled the contents of his glass into Abe's face. Letting out a startled yelp, the hard-case retreated a few steps. Abe's hands rose in an involuntary gesture as the raw liquor stung his eyes and his gun went off to send its bullet harmlessly into the ceiling. Ignoring Abe after throwing the whiskey, Svenson hurled himself to the left. Ramming his shoulder into Harpe, he knocked the guerilla staggering. At the same moment, seizing his opportunity, the hotel's owner dropped out of sight behind the counter.

From throwing Monte over his shoulder, Dusty straightened his bent leg and thrust himself erect. While spinning around to face the bar, he noticed that Gilbertson had snatched up Monte's Starr revolver and was coming to his feet. Satisfied that the Yankee would honour his parole, Dusty expected that he would use the gun to help fight off the guerillas. So Dusty concentrated his attention on dealing with the gambler's companions. He saw Svenson charging into Harpe, but knew that the affair had not yet ended.

Still reeling from the impact, Harpe cut loose with a

shot in Dusty's direction. Lead screamed eerily by the small Texan's head, coming so close that it gave warning of the hard-case's ability. A man with such skill was too dangerous to be trifled with.

Dusty sent his hands flashing across his body. Like twin extensions of his will, the matched Colts left their holsters. Passing each other with smooth precision, the seven-and-one-half inch long Civilian Model barrels* turned outwards and pointed at Harpe. Before the guns had cleared leather, their hammers were thumbed back to the full-cock position. Once the barrels started to turn, Dusty's forefingers entered the trigger guards. So all was ready the instant the Colts lined at his target.

From waist high, aimed by instinctive alignment, the Colts went off in what sounded like a single crash. Three-quarters of a second after Dusty's hands had made their first movements, two 219-grain bullets were speeding towards Harpe. Both struck him in the forehead with less than an inch separating them. Flung backwards, the guerilla collided with the bar and bounced lifeless from it to the floor.

While the smoke still swirled from his guns, a sudden impact from behind knocked Dusty reeling. With an effort, he managed to maintain his hold on the two Colts. Fighting to regain his balance and avoid falling, he heard the sound of running feet to his rear and twisted to look over his shoulder.

About to turn back and deal with Abe, after watching Dusty take Harpe out of the game, Svenson saw Gilbertson lunge from his chair. Dropping his right shoulder, the Yan-

* The standard-size Army Colt had an eight inch barrel.

kee officer charged the small Texan from the rear. Having knocked Dusty out of the way, the Volunteer bounded across the room. It was clear that, despite having given his word, he intended to escape.

Letting out an angry bellow, Svenson sprang to meet the fleeing man. No gunfighter, the blond recruit lacked the coordination and fast reactions required to draw a gun with blinding speed. In a fight, he much preferred to use his big fists. So he plunged resolutely in Gilbertson's direction and made no attempt to reach for his holstered revolver.

Even when he had given it, Gilbertson had no intention of keeping his parole. He had planned to take advantage of his escort relaxing their vigilance, on accepting his word, and to escape during the night. To make certain of reaching safety, he would need a horse. Learning that Dusty was putting two men to guard the party's mounts had caused Gilbertson's hopes to dwindle. The intervention of Monte's guerillas had opened another avenue of departure for him.

Acting more on blind impulse than a thought-out plan, Gilbertson had not used the Starr to remove Dusty from his path. By the time the idea of doing so had come to him, he had knocked the small Texan aside and gone running by. To turn and shoot would waste valuable seconds; especially when the second of the guerillas might kill the Rebel captain for him. At that moment too, the stocky blond recruit presented a greater threat to Gilbertson's bid for freedom.

Throwing forward the Starr, the Volunteer pressed its trigger. Back rode the double-action hammer, then slammed forward. A .44 bullet ripped into the centre of Svenson's chest, halting his advance. Involuntarily Gilbertson relaxed his forefinger and tightened it again. The Starr spat at the height of its recoil kick, sending its next load into the centre of Svenson's forehead. Knocked from his feet, the recruit no longer impeded Gilbertson's flight. Without giving his victim a second glance, the Volunteer ran on.

Digging in with his heels, Dusty came to a halt and started to swing in Gilbertson's direction. Hot anger blazed inside the small Texan at the Volunteer's treachery. Even as Dusty prepared to lunge in pursuit, a gun roared from the left side stairs and its bullet stirred his hair in passing.

Throwing himself aside in a rolling dive, Dusty saw Will coming down the stairs. Smoke curled from the revolver in the man's hand and he had miraculously lost his limp. There was no time to think about that. Landing on the floor, Dusty cut loose with first left, then right hand Colt. Through the swirling clouds of discharged gas that belched out of the muzzles, he saw Will jolt as if struck by an invisible hand. Falling backwards, Will sat down, then slid to the floor of the stairs. The Colt slipped from his hand as he came to a stop.

Turning onto his stomach, Dusty saw his prisoner leaping through the front door. Before the small Texan could make another movement, he heard the blast of detonating gunpowder. Splinters erupted from the planks ahead of him. Twirling himself over so that he could look in the direction from which the shot had come, Dusty saw Abe looming towards him. Again the man fired, but his whiskey-inflamed eyes and the haste of his actions did not lend to accurate sighting. Another hole appeared in the floor, less than a foot from the side of Dusty's head.

Trained thumbs drew back the Colts' hammers as Dusty continued to roll over. He squeezed the triggers while on his back and with the revolvers extended at arms' length above his head. Shock twisted the rage from the guerilla's face as two bullets tore through his rib-cage. Spinning in a circle, he released his hold on his weapon and stumbled away from it to collapse face down.

Completing his roll, Dusty wasted no time in regaining his feet. Yet, fast as he moved, he knew that he might still be too late. From the street came the snorting of disturbed horses and, farther away, shouts rang out. Running towards the window, Dusty noticed that Monte was recovering and rolling painfully back and forwards on the table.

Ignoring the gambler, Dusty watched what was happening outside the building. Already Gilbertson had swung astride the best of the horses fiddle-footing nervously at the hitching-rail. Up swung the Starr, crashing twice in concert with the Volunteer's wild and ringing yell. All too well Dusty saw the other's plan. With their own horses unsaddled at the livery barn, the Texans might still have launched a rapid pursuit using the remaining guerillas' mounts. So Gilbertson intended to run them off and put them beyond the reach of the Rebels. Swinging his borrowed horse around by savagely tugging at the reins, the Volunteer started it moving. Already disturbed, the other animals scattered and fled into the night.

Spitting out furious curses, Dusty hurled himself towards the window. Behind him, the hotel's owner had made a cautious reappearance and wailed a protest as his intentions became apparent. Paying no attention to the man, Dusty covered his head with his arms and propelled himself from the building by the closest route. Glass shattered and wood crackled as Dusty passed through the window. Landing on the sidewalk, he swung his right hand Colt to shoulder level. He sighted as well as he could at the fast-moving, already barely-discernible rider. More in hope than expectancy, Dusty squeezed off a shot. Even as the recoil kicked the barrel upwards, he knew that he had missed.

Boots drumming a rapid tattoo along the sidewalk,

Kiowa, Prince and Graveling raced up. They all held their guns, but had no target at which to aim. Gilbertson had gone from sight.

"What the hell——?" Kiowa began.

"Gilbertson ran out!" Dusty spat back. "Let's go inside. The son-of-a-bitch shot Ollie Svenson."

Turning without further chatter, the enlisted men followed Dusty through the hotel's front door. On entering the barroom, they saw the gambler straightening up with Will's Colt in his hand. Snarling in mixed fear and fury, Monte tried to turn his acquired weapon on the newcomers. Six revolvers roared in a ragged volley, Dusty and Prince each carrying one in either hand. Literally lifted from his feet and hurled backwards by the bullets, any one of which would have been fatal, the gambler crumpled lifeless in the left rear corner of the room.

"That's the last of them!" Dusty said with savage bitterness. "See to Ollie."

Holstering his revolver, Graveling walked over and made a brief examination of the body. Looking to where the rest of the Texans were replacing their guns into leather, he gave a resigned shrug.

"He's cashed in."

"What happened?" Prince demanded truculently. "How did——?"

"No chance of following the Yankee, Cap'n Dusty," Kiowa put in, glaring a furious warning that silenced the recruit. "Not afore morning, anyways."

"None," Dusty agreed. "But I want to be on his trail as soon as it's daylight, Kiowa."

"He'll be over the Caddo afore then!" Prince protested.

"I don't care where the hell he is!" Dusty replied and the young recruit began to feel an awareness of his personality's full deadly powerful force. "Gilbertson broke his parole and killed one of my friends. I aim to fetch him back."

Straightening up after a long, careful examination of a set of hoof-marks, Kiowa turned and walked to where Dusty, Prince and Surtees were waiting for him. The sun had only barely lifted above the eastern horizon, but the sergeant-scout had been out at the first glint of light and following his commanding officer's orders.

"I'd say these're the right 'n's, Cap'n Dusty," Kiowa declared. "They're the right age, anyways, and toting a rider."

"Trouble being they're not headed towards the Caddo," Dusty pointed out. Twisting in his saddle, he looked back at the town of Amity. "It's the way Gilbertson came out, though."

If the incident had taken place the previous day, Tracey Prince would have been crowding forward and inserting his views on the matter. Sitting his horse at the rear of the party, as became its most junior and inexperienced member, he waited to discover what Captain Fog and the lean, Indian-dark sergeant intended to do. Already aware of Kiowa Cotton's competence before they had left Prescott, Prince was becoming more and more convinced that he had been wrong in dismissing Dusty Fog as a rich kid put into power by his kinfolk.

For all his cocky attitude and believing that he was so wild he had never been curried below the knees, Prince possessed enough common-sense to realise he had gone as far as he could without forcing an open showdown between himself and Dusty. Although he fought against admitting it, his instincts also warned him that he might regret the result if a clash came. He had seen and heard enough the previous night to tell him that Dusty Fog was far more than Ole Devil Hardin's nephew wearing a captain's coat.

After Svenson's body had been removed from the barroom, Prince had watched the coldly efficient manner in which Dusty had handled the rest of the situation. While the small Texan and Kiowa had accompanied the town constable to inspect the dead guerillas' rooms, the hotel's owner had delivered a graphic description to Prince and the assembled townsmen of what had happened.

The story of how Dusty had so easily tossed the bulky gambler over his shoulder had drawn excited comments from the civilians. Prince had been less impressed, for he had seen that side of his captain's ability demonstrated. What started the recruit's change of heart had been the visual proof of Dusty's gun-fighting potential.

Svenson had been killed with his gun still in leather. Certainly the Yankee officer had played no part in the fight beyond shooting down the blond recruit. That meant Dusty Fog must have come through the corpse-and-cartridge affair unaided and against three men. More to the point, he had killed two and critically wounded the third of his assailants. Prince had sufficient knowledge of shooting to imagine the deadly gun-skill required to ensure survival under those exacting conditions.

Yet there had been more to Dusty Fog than just fast, accurate and effective lead-throwing. Prince had received further evidence of his Company commander's dynamic personality as he watched how Dusty had handled the irate owner of the hotel. At first the man had been nervous and inclined to righteous indignation; nervous over how his Army-guests would regard his part—or lack of it—in the affair, and indignant about the damage suffered by his property.

Without threats or recriminations, Dusty had calmed

and soothed the man. He had, on his return from searching the guerillas' property, stated that he did not hold the owner responsible for the incident; which had been a relief to the man. On the subject of the shattered window, Dusty had pointed out that the dead guerilla's belongings and such of their horses as might be recovered ought to more than pay for its replacement.

A shrewd businessman, the owner had seen the wisdom of not pressing his complaints farther. If he did so, he would certainly antagonise a member of the most powerful faction in West Arkansas. Thinking deeper into the affair, the owner could also see how his business might benefit from it. Every instinct the owner possessed had told him that the young captain might, most likely would, attain some prominence in the future. So the hotel could attract customers by being the scene of an incident involving him. With that in mind, the owner had announced that he did not blame Captain Fog for the trouble or the damage.

Borrowing a pen, ink and writing paper, Dusty had made out a report of the incident. At least, Prince assumed that was what his captain had written. Whatever it had been, Dusty had given the completed document to Graveling and issued orders for its delivery to the Regiment's headquarters. A hard-case, with a reputation for salty toughness, Graveling's unspoken acceptance of the orders had been a further subject of thought for Prince. After making arrangements for Svenson's funeral, the Texans had turned in.

Before daylight that morning, Dusty and his men had been preparing to move out. Graveling had come to see them off and been told to attend the funeral, then return to Prescott as quickly as he could.

Now a chastened, slightly perturbed Prince sat watching Dusty Fog and awaiting the next development.

"We'll see where these tracks go," Dusty decided.

"Yo!" Kiowa replied.

Collecting his horse from Surtees, the sergeant went afork it with a bound. Dusty nudged his stallion's ribs with his heels and gave the order to move out. With his eyes raking the ground ahead, Kiowa took the lead. Following the tracks of a single horse over short, springy grass and through lightly-wooded country could not be done at speed. So the party moved slowly and in a westerly direction.

After covering about a mile, Dusty could sense the two privates' doubts and knew what caused them. In fact, while he had complete faith in Kiowa's ability to read sign, he began to wonder if maybe they were following the wrong set of tracks.

"Feller stopped there," Kiowa remarked, bringing his horse to a halt and pointing ahead. "Then he turned around a couple of times, like he was trying to figure which way he was headed."

"What'd he decide?" Dusty inquired.

"Moved off to the north," Kiowa replied.

"That'd take him to Caddo," Dusty said.

"Sure would," Kiowa agreed. "Giddap, hoss!"

Starting their mounts moving, they followed the tracks but had not covered more than a hundred yards before Kiowa stopped them again.

"He's swinging off to the west again, Cap'n Dusty."

"Could be he's lost. That'd happen easy enough. A man could soon get himself all turned around in this sort of country on a dark night."

"A dude like that Yankee could," Kiowa admitted. "And if he's lost, maybe we'll find him."

"We can hope on it," Dusty drawled.

The hope did not materialise. After wavering from side

to side and changing direction twice in the next half a mile, the rider had stopped and made camp for the night. Clearly he had wasted no time in getting his bearings at sun-up, for he had already moved off in the correct direction if he wanted to reach the Caddo River.

"He's not more'n an hour and a half ahead," Kiowa commented as they took up the trail again. "What do we do now, Cap'n Dusty, see if we can ride him down?"

"Nope. Not with that much of a lead on us," Dusty replied. "He'll be over the Caddo before we can do it."

For the first time that morning, Prince put in a question. When he spoke, his voice held little of its earlier arrogant near-insolence.

"What'll we do if he licks us to the river and goes over, Cap'n?"

"We'll go after him," Dusty stated flatly.

"It'll be near on two days afore the Company can get here," Prince pointed out. "By that time——"

"We won't be waiting for the Company," Dusty interrupted quietly, then turned his attention to the front.

"Don't let it worry you, soldier," Surtees said quietly as Prince turned a startled face his way. "Cap'n Dusty's likely got something in mind."

Prince decided against asking what it might be. If Kiowa and the bugler were willing to accompany the small captain, the recruit did not mean to let them think that he felt concern for his own safety. For all that, he was puzzled and worried by the thought of what might lie ahead.

A yearning for excitement and adventure had brought Tracey Prince into the Texas Light Cavalry. On joining, he had expected to be sent straight into the battle front and had seen himself winning instantaneous acclaim for his courage against the Yankees. Instead of being accepted as the finished product he had believed himself to be, he had been treated as a raw hand. During his training, he had repeatedly bewailed the waste of time learning how to drill and do other fool soldier tricks. He had regarded his arrival in Company "C" as the prelude to action and had looked forward eagerly to coming to grips with the enemy.

Yet, never in his wildest daydreams, had he conceived that he would be part of such an expedition. Beyond the Caddo River lay Yankee-held territory. Sure the Texas Light Cavalry raided across it regularly—but at Company strength. He felt certain that, as a general rule, a group of no more than four men did not go beyond the boundary river.

All the time they were riding, Prince scanned the land ahead of them in the hope of seeing the escaped Yankee. The woods through which they passed grew thicker and he saw no sign of Gilbertson. At last Prince caught a glimpse of water glinting through the trees and Kiowa signalled to them to halt. Quietly Dusty gave the order to dismount. Swinging to the ground, Dusty allowed his split-end reins to fall free. Doing so held a range-trained horse as effectively as tying it to a branch.

"Tracks keep going down there, Cap'n," Kiowa announced as Dusty joined him. "Likely he went straight across. Do we head after him?"

"Take a look around first," Dusty advised. "If he met up with a Yankee patrol, they could figure we'll be following and be laying up for us when we try to go across."

Leaving his horse ground-hitched by its trailing reins, Kiowa glided off through the trees. Dusty and the two privates waited in silence, watching how the sergeant took advantage of every scrap of cover during his approach to the river's edge.

While his men raked the opposite shore with an intent

scrutiny, Dusty studied his surroundings and estimated their position on the Caddo. Unless he missed his guess, they were about two miles downstream from the Snake Ford. He knew which of Buller's regiments currently had the responsibility of patrolling that area of the river. Making use of his knowledge, Dusty formulated a plan for repossessing the absconding Volunteer. He did not tell his companions of his intentions, figuring that they would have doubts as to the chance of his bringing it off.

Almost half an hour went by before Kiowa returned. Nothing showed on his brown, hard features, but Dusty knew the sergeant had not liked what lay ahead.

"He went straight across, Cap'n Dusty. Not more'n an hour ago."

"Have we anybody waiting for us?"

"Not as I could see," Kiowa admitted. "Only it's real thick bushes over the other side."

"And they could be laying for us?" Dusty asked.

"Could be," Kiowa drawled. "There's places enough for 'em to hide and me not to see 'em."

"It's a chance I'll have to take," Dusty decided, then turned to the two privates. "This's as far as I'm ordering you to come."

"Happen you're asking for volunteers, Cap'n Dusty," Surtees answered laconically, "I'm game to give it a whirl."

"And me!" Prince went on, hoping that his voice showed none of the perturbation he felt.

Cautiously, leading their horses, the Texans wended their way towards the river. All of them gave the opposite bank their full attention, probing it for any sign of lurking enemies. They halted just before reaching the narrow path that followed the course of the river, worn by the boots and hooves of many Confederate patrols, without obtaining conclusive evidence for or against there being Yankees waiting to ambush them.

"There's only one way to make sure," Dusty declared. "I'm going over." He looked at Kiowa, then to Surtees and finally in Prince's direction, continuing, "Feel like coming with me, soldier?"

The words came as a shock to Prince and he did not answer for a moment. Then he realised that Dusty had called him "soldier" instead of the coldly-formal "Prince."

Was there a hint of challenge in the request?

"I'm with you, Cap'n," Prince decided, trying to sound far more nonchalant than he was feeling.

For all his light-hearted comment, Dusty had no intention of advancing blindly into danger. Before starting, there were certain precautions to be taken.

"Here's my Henry, Kiowa," Dusty drawled, reaching forward to slide the repeating rifle—a battlefield capture —from its saddle-boot, then handing it over. "You and the bugler'd best cover us. If we don't make it, head back and tell Uncle Devil what's happened."

"Yo!" Kiowa answered calmly, hefting the Henry. "The current's fast, but it's not too deep where he went over. You should get through without swimming."

"We'll make sure of dry guns, anyway," Dusty decided.

Unbuckling their belts, Dusty and Prince suspended them across their shoulders so as to try to keep the Colts from becoming wet. Drawing his Enfield rifle, Surtees checked that its percussion cap was intact and adjusted the sights. Then he and Kiowa watched their companions mount up and ride towards the river.

"Young Prince looked a mite peaked," Surtees commented *sotte voce*, never taking his eyes from the other bank. "He went with Cap'n Dusty game enough, though."

"Why sure," Kiowa agreed. "He'll make a hand—happen he comes through this, that is."

If Prince had heard the two veterans' words, they would have given him pleasure by their implication of acceptance into the elite ranks of Company "C." However, at that moment the recruit had far too much on his mind to be interested in his companions' good opinions of him. Crossing the path, the horses splashed into the water and moved steadily forward.

Ahead the woods still lay silent. The trees, bushes and grass looked no different to those which they had just left. For all that, Prince knew the woodland on the eastern bank was different.

Very, *very* different!

Menacingly and dangerously so!

To the rear were friends and comparative safety. Ahead of Prince and Dusty, the Yankees dominated the whole eastern side of the Caddo. Even now, blue-clad soldiers might be peering and leering along the barrels of Springfield rifles at the two intruders.

Prince ran the tip of his tongue across lips that suddenly felt dry.

"Was you ever in Arkansas before the War, Tracey?" Dusty inquired, without relaxing his vigilance.

"N-Nope!" Prince croaked, startled by hearing the small Texan's voice rather than at the question.

"Or me," Dusty admitted. "Seen a fair bit of it since the War started, though. Trouble is I've still not met Annie Breen."

"Huh?" Prince gulped.

Although he had already started to make his name as a

lady's man, which would eventually be the cause of his death,* for once the mention of a woman brought little of Prince's usual eager response.

"According to the song, she lived out this way," Dusty elaborated. "Or was it from Kentucky?"

"Wha——?"

"How's the song go,
        "Come all you lads of Arkansas,

        To you a tale I bring,
        Of Annie Breen from old Kaintuck—"

"Hell, there's no wonder I've never run across her."

Swivelling his eyes from the bank ahead, Prince stared at the small Texan for a moment. It seemed impossible that an experienced soldier, riding into possible danger, could think about the words of a folk song.

The force of the current's thrust compelled Prince to return his attention to the horse between his legs. However, underfoot the firm gravel of the river's bed offered a safe footing and the animals found little difficulty in wading. Returning his gaze hurriedly to the eastern shore, Prince stiffened in his saddle.

Was that a rifle's barrel, black and evil-looking, thrusting its way out of a clump of dogwood bushes?

"Anyways," Dusty's voice came quiet and unconcernedly to Prince's ears. "I don't reckon it'd be worth meeting her now. That song was written back in the 'forties. She'd be a heap too old for either of us. Easy, it's only a branch."

A faint sigh of relief broke from the recruit. For all the

---

* How is told in *The Bad Bunch*.

flow of carefree chatter, his captain was also watching what lay ahead.

By that time they had almost reached the centre of the river. The water had risen nearly to the tops of the saddles' rosaderos,† but came no higher. By raising their feet from the stirrup-irons, the riders avoided wetting their boots. Doing so called for a careful watch to be kept on one's balance and for a short time it held Prince's full attention.

As the level of the water subsided, the recruit returned his feet to the stirrups and resumed his scrutiny of the woodland. Darting his eyes back and forwards, Prince saw what he thought was a man spread-eagled behind a rock. Close examination showed it to be a fallen tree-trunk.

Or was it?

Captain Fog had stopped his horse and was reaching towards his gunbelt!

With a feeling of shock, Prince reined in his mount. Instinctively his right hand dropped towards his hip—to feel nothing more protective than the material of his breeches' leg.

"Nobody around after all," Dusty remarked. "But we'd better strap on our belts now. Then we'll be set to cover Kiowa and Surtees while they come over."

"Yo!" Prince replied, hoping that his commanding officer had not noticed his involuntary gesture.

Lowering their gunbelts to the more usual position about their waists, Dusty and Prince connected the buckles. With that done, they started their horses moving. Prince could not prevent himself sucking in a deep anticipatory breath as he followed the small Texan. Ascending the gentle incline

† Rosaderos: wide, vertical shields stitched to the back of the stirrup leathers.

of the eastern bank, they crossed the trail that had been enlarged by Federal patrols and went into the thick undergrowth beyond it.

With a cold, sinking sensation biting into his stomach, Prince realised that he was now inside enemy territory. The fact that he was the first of his recruit-intake to get there never occurred to him. His full attention was given to staring around. At any moment, he expected to see hordes of Yankee soldiers swarming in his direction.

Glancing sideways, Prince was impressed by Dusty's attitude of calm, detached alertness. The small captain, whom Prince had previously been inclined to deride—if only silently—had clearly made such crossings many times and regarded them as commonplace. It was comforting to know that one served under so competent and courageous an officer. From that moment, Tracey Prince joined the ranks of the many who regarded Dusty Fog as being the tallest of them all.

Having taken up concealed positions among the bushes, Dusty told Prince to keep a watch on the upstream section of the trail. Then he waved to the men on the other side. Joining the advance party, Kiowa and Surtees flashed cheery, friendly grins at Prince.

"You handled that just like a veteran," the bugler praised.

"Better," Dusty corrected. "Us young 'n's don't have you veterans' creaking old bones to slow us. And I'll have the Henry, Kiowa. That's how I got it."

"Never did have time for no Yankee metal-case gun, anyways," the sergeant sniffed, returning the rifle. "Give me something I can get fodder for."

"Where'd Gilbertson come out, if it's him we're trailing?"

"Upstream a mite, Cap'n."

"Let's go get him," Dusty ordered, retaining the Henry in his right hand.

Flushed with pride at the knowledge that he had won his companions' approbation, Prince watched the sergeant move a short way along the river's bank. Dropping from his saddle, Kiowa bent and picked up something that his keen eyes had detected as it lay half concealed in the mud at the edge of the water. Signalling to the others to join him, he held his find towards Dusty.

"He must've dropped it as he come out of the river, Cap'n," the sergeant guessed. "Likely he didn't want to chance stopping to pick it up."

"It" proved to be a Starr Army revolver, covered with mud. Taking it, Dusty found that four of the chambers had been emptied.

"Or figured he wouldn't be likely to need it again," Dusty replied with satisfaction. The discovery of the Starr had given them the first real proof that they were following the right tracks. "It's the gun he used to kill Ollie Svenson."

"He ain't sticking to the trail, though," Kiowa observed, indicating the evidence that somebody, or something, had forced a path through the bushes.

"That figures," Dusty answered. "If he had, he might've been seen by one of our patrols. He'd want to get into cover rather than chance that."

"Yeah," Kiowa agreed.

Turning their horses in the direction taken by the man they were following, the Texans rode on. Their way led them through the thick woodlands which flanked the Caddo at that point, then into the more open, rolling country.

"He's not turning to go up to the Snake Ford," Kiowa remarked, letting Dusty come alongside his horse.

"I wasn't expecting him to," Dusty admitted. "Way he left us, he'll not want to go there and be asked questions."

With each stride, the horses carried their riders deeper into enemy-held terrain. Prince felt his tension rising again as he kept up a constant surveillance of his surroundings. Watching the flanks, he forgot to look ahead. He had his attention drawn forcibly in that direction as Kiowa once more brought the party to a halt. Staring in the line indicated by the sergeant's pointing forefinger, Prince stiffened and gulped. Several thin columns of smoke rose from beyond a rim about a mile in front of them. From what the recruits saw, the tracks they were following went towards the smoke.

"What do you reckon, Kiowa?" Dusty inquired.

"Company of 'em at least," the sergeant replied. "And this here's the 'New Jersey' Dragoons' stomping grounds."

That had been one of the factors taken into consideration by the small Texan before he led the way across the river. The 6th "New Jersey" Dragoons was a regular Army regiment, commanded by career officers. Most efficient of all Buller's outfits, the Dragoons were one Yankee force in Arkansas that even the Texas Light Cavalry regarded as dangerous.

"Take a point, Kiowa," Dusty ordered. "If that's where Gilbertson's going, so're we."

Allowing Kiowa to build up a lead of almost a hundred yards, Dusty started the remainder of the party moving. Prince looked at the smoke-columns, trying to estimate how many men had been responsible for making them. While he could not decide upon an accurate figure, he felt certain that his own group would be heavily outnumbered. That the man they were following was heading towards the smoke grew more positive by the minute. Watching the *big* captain, Prince wondered what he hoped to accomplish with a sergeant and two privates if Gilbertson had joined up with a large number of Dragoons.

Ranging ahead of the others, Kiowa kept an especially keen watch for the Dragoons' vedettes and pickets. If the men ahead had been in camp for a day or longer, they would have taken such defensive precautions. He saw none and at last dismounted, leaving his horse ground-hitched while he continued up the slope on foot. Flattening down on his stomach, he crawled the last few feet and peered cautiously over the rim from behind a bush. What he saw explained away the Dragoons' lack of guards around their campsite. Moving back with equal care, the sergeant returned to his patiently-waiting horse.

"It's a full company of 'em, Cap'n Dusty," Kiowa reported. "They're just finishing packing and'll be pulling out soon."

Listening to the softly-spoken, unemotional words, Prince decided that they would trail along after the Dragoons and try to sneak Gilbertson out of the Yankees' next night camp. It would not be easy——

"Is he with 'em?" Dusty asked, cutting across the recruit's thoughts.

"Yep," confirmed the sergeant. "He's there. I saw him stood talking to the Dragoons' major."

"What're we going to do now, Cap'n Dusty?" Surtees inquired.

"Go and get him back," Dusty replied and handed his Henry to Kiowa.

"You mean you're aiming to ride over that rim and *ask* the Yankees to give him back?" Prince gasped, watching the small Texan unbuckle his gunbelt.

"Nope," Dusty said, quietly but with determination. "I'm going to *tell* them to hand him over."

Crystal clear in the morning air, the notes of a bugle-call rang out from the rim overlooking the campsite used the previous night by Troop "G" of the 6th "New Jersey" Dragoons. Having been pulled in for breakfast, the men from the vedettes and pickets were sitting around the dying fires instead of being stationed about the surrounding area. The remainder of the Troop stood with their horses in four files, being inspected by the captain and two lieutenants.

Startled exclamations burst from the enlisted men and officers as they looked in the direction from which the call sounded. Then eyes turned towards the piles of Springfield carbines, left stacked while their owners completed the final tasks of breaking camp, and the soldiers gave thought to their holstered revolvers.

"Blasted Rebs!" yelped a young soldier, jerking open his holster's flap.

"Leave it be, son," ordered the grizzled veteran at his side, watching without any concern as two riders approached down the slope. "They're coming in to make a parley."

"What the hell?" demanded Major Galbraith, swinging away from Gilbertson and examining the cause of the disturbance. "Take up defensive positions, men!"

Swiftly, with the efficient, purposeful actions of well-trained troops, the Dragoons sprang to obey. Each section of four left its horses in the care of one man and the other three erupted into motion. Pyramids of carbines disintegrated with disciplined speed. Gripping their saddle-guns, urged on by barked-out commands from the officers, the Dragoons fanned out and took up positions which would allow them to meet an attack from any side. Dropping to the ground in whatever cover they could find, the enlisted men swung their carbines into firing postures.

"No shooting, men!" Captain Miller called and the noncommissioned officers repeated the warning.

Major Galbraith watched his men assume a state of all-round defence and nodded his approval. If the surly Volunteer at his side knew anything about military matters, he would be impressed by the Dragoons' efficiency. With that thought come and gone, Galbraith turned his attention to the approaching pair of riders. A long-serving career-officer, the major recognised the significance of what he saw.

Going by the "chicken guts" on his sleeve, the small, young-looking man at the left was an officer. In his right hand, he carried a rifle's ramrod to which a white bandana had been fastened like a flag. Raising a bugle to his lips, the second rider blew another loud call on it. Neither of the newcomers appeared to be carrying arms of any kind.

That was the traditional, established procedure for requesting a truce or a parley. The white flag and lack of weapons announced the two men's pacific intentions, while the repeated bugle calls proved that they did not mean to surprise the enemy soldiers.

Dishevelled, unshaven and bleary-eyed, Gilbertson stared up the slope in horror. At first he could hardly believe that he was awake and felt that he must be dreaming. Recognising the newcomers, he felt a growing sense of foreboding. Spitting out a low, savage curse, he dropped his right hand across to close on the hilt of his sabre.

"Is something wrong, Captain Gilbertson?" asked the tall, lean, leathery-faced major as he became aware of the Volunteer's perturbation.

Taking warning from the Dragoon's tone, Gilbertson held down a reply which he had been about to give. Instead he nodded in the direction of the Texans and said, "You've got a good catch here, Major."

"I don't follow you," Galbraith growled.

"That's young Fog," elaborated the Volunteer. "Hardin's nephew."

"And that's a white flag he's carrying," the Dragoon pointed out coldly. "So I'll hear what he has to say." Looking around, Galbraith raised his voice. "Stand to your arms, men. Captain Miller, Mr. Coulson, Mr. Hargrove, make sure that nobody opens fire unless the Rebs make a hostile move."

"Yo!" came the answer from the Troop's subordinate officers.

Squaring his shoulders, Galbraith set the peaked Dragoon forage cap straighter on his head. Another sweeping glance around the campsite assured him that all was ready, in case—which he doubted—the Confederate soldiers planned some treachery. If they did, they would meet with a hot, and well-deserved, reception. Satisfied, he strode forward and passed through his Troop's defensive circle. Filled with curiosity, and fears for his own safety, Gilbertson followed the major.

Young, insignificant almost in appearance, or not, the Confederate captain knew military convention and etiquette. Coming to a halt at least a hundred yards from the nearest defender, so that he could not see too many details of their armament and disposition, he handed the white flag to his bugler. Dismounting, he left his black stallion with its reins dangling free and advanced a further fifty feet on foot. Coming to a halt before the Yankees, he threw up a smart salute directed at Galbraith.

"Fog. Captain. Texas Light Cavalry, sir," Dusty announced formally as the Dragoon returned his salute.

"Major Galbraith, 6th 'New Jersey' Dragoons," the senior of the two Federal officers acknowledged, then indicated the man hovering behind him. "This is——"

"I know who he is, sir," Dusty interrupted politely but

coldly. "Captain Gilbertson was my prisoner——"

"And he escaped?"

"No, sir. He ran away after giving me his word of honour that he *wouldn't* escape. So I've come to take him back. Will you order him to get ready, please."

"What's this?" Galbraith barked, swinging furiously to glare at Gilbertson. "Is it true?"

Not that the Dragoon needed to ask, or to see the guilt on the Volunteer's face, to know the answer. Ever since Gilbertson had arrived that morning, Galbraith had grown increasingly doubtful of his veracity. The captain had spun a reasonably convincing story of his carefully-planned and executed escape from Murfreesboro, but there had been points left unexplained in the telling. One of them being how he had regained possession of his sword. It would have been taken from him at his capture, to be held by the Rebels until his release.

Of course, a man who had won the admiration and respect of his enemies might have his sword returned as a tribute to his courage or ability. Gilbertson did not strike the hard-bitten Galbraith as being that kind of officer. Nor would he have had, in the Dragoon's opinion, sufficient notions of honour to take the chances involved in gaining possession of his sword before escaping.

Captain Fog's words had confirmed Galbraith's suspicions, although the Dragoon had fought against the one answer that would have explained everything. More than that, they had placed an entirely different complexion on Gilbertson's presence. Any officer who escaped from captivity by fair means deserved praise and approbation. That did not apply to the methods by which the sullen Volunteer had attained his freedom.

"Damn it, Gilbertson!" Galbraith blazed when the Volunteer did not answer. "Is this true, or isn't it?"

"It's true, sir," Dusty put in. "Last night in the hotel at Amity, he gave his word, in the presence of my bugler, not to escape before dawn."

"In Amity?" Galbraith growled.

"Yes, sir. I was escorting him to the Snake Ford to be exchanged for one of our captains. We had a run-in with some guerillas and during the fighting, he killed one of my men and ran. I've come to take him back."

Being fully aware of guerillas' habits, Galbraith could guess that the Texans had been fighting to protect their prisoner. Which only made Gilbertson's actions the more reprehensible.

"Well?" the Dragoon spat at the Volunteer.

"All right," Gilbertson snarled. "So I saw my chance and took it."

The calm admission struck Galbraith dumb for a moment. He could hardly believe that an officer in the United States' Army would brazenly make such a confession. In fact, the Dragoon did not want to believe it. So he sought desperately for some excuse or mitigating circumstance— even though he doubted if there could be one against such a charge.

"You understood what you were doing when you gave your word?" the major demanded, hoping that the other would answer in the negative.

"Of course I did!" Gilbertson yelped, his college-educated superiority revolting at the suggestion that there might be something he did not know.

"And after giving your word," Galbraith breathed, "you still ran?"

"I'd every intention of running, that's why I gave it," Gilbertson declared. "What the hell do you think war is, some kind of game to be played by rules?"

"You'll have to go back!" Galbraith stated.

"If he was stupid enough to thi——" Gilbertson continued, then the full implication of the Dragoon's words penetrated his mind. The flow of bombastic rhetoric gurgled to an uneven halt and he stared in amazement at the cold-faced, angry major. "Wha-wha——?"

"You'll have to go back with Captain Fog," Galbraith elaborated grimly. "Damn it all, man. If you don't care about your own honour, think of how this action of yours will look in the eyes of the world. The Union Army—the whole United States—will stand condemned unless you go back."

"Who'll know about it?" Gilbertson asked scornfully. "My father will see that Buller hushes it up."

"*I*'ll know, for one," Galbraith pointed out. "And so will Captain Fog."

A deep, bitter sense of frustrated fury tore at Gilbertson. Filled with the arrogant, egotistical self-importance of the "liberal-intellectual" college student, he had entered the Union Army certain that his superlative brilliance must destine him for great deeds. Like many another of his kind, he had found himself sadly lacking in practical knowledge once faced with the harsh realities of life. So he had failed to achieve even a modicum of success in a field which he had always regarded as being the province of men with limited intelligence.

To have been captured by the despised Rebels, in his first essay at active duty, had rankled and hurt. Especially as it had been through his own stupidity and inefficiency that he had fallen into their hands. To know that he was gaining his liberty at the expense of freeing one of the hated Southerners had been an intolerable humiliation.

Not that he had thought of refusing the offer, or passing

it to one of his companions in Murfreesboro. Such a sac-
rifice was not in keeping with his small-minded, self-
centered nature.

He had already been thinking of escape during the journey to the Snake Ford. Seeing the youth and general insig-
nificance of his escort's leader, he had felt sure that
slipping away could be accomplished with no difficulty.
Doing so would reassert his sense of self-importance, hu-
miliate Ole Devil Hardin, and prevent the Rebel prisoner
from attaining freedom.

Being fully aware of the convention of war concerning
an officer's parole, Gilbertson had intended to make use of
it. Even if that short-grown Texan had not suggested a
truce until dawn, the Volunteer had meant to do so. Gilbertson had seen his opportunity in the Amity hotel, taken
it and had finally reached what ought to have been safety.

Then that infernal Rebel captain had appeared and demanded—not asked, *demanded!*—that he be returned.

To make matters worse, Galbraith—a stinking career
officer—clearly intended to comply with the small Texan's
wishes.

Gilbertson's full, bigoted hatred reached a boiling point
as he considered the lousy trick fate had played on him. To
have escaped, found his way across the Caddo, then to
have fallen in with a lousy, stupid career officer who believed in conventions and out-moded codes of honour.

"Him!" the Volunteer screeched, throwing a glare of
loathing at Dusty. "Who the hell cares what a lousy Secessionist peckerwood* thinks?"

"*I* care," Galbraith barked and turned his back on Gilbertson as he addressed the Confederate officer. "Captain

* Peckerwood: derogatory name for a white Southerner.

Fog, I apologise on behalf of the United States Army and——"

Wild with rage, fear and near panic, Gilbertson slid the sabre from its sheath. If he killed the Rebel officer, he would present Galbraith with a *fait accompli*. The Dragoon major would have to conceal the fact that the incident had happened, if only to preserve the honour of his sacred Union Army. With Gilbertson's father so influential in New Hampstead affairs, General Buller could be counted on to prevent too close an inquiry into the matter. In fact, Buller would exert his authority as the commanding general in Arkansas to prevent any military disciplinary action being invoked against Gilbertson.

So the Volunteer believed that he had nothing to lose and everything to gain if he killed Dusty Fog. Having attended fencing classes in college, Gilbertson knew he could handle the sabre well enough to dispatch an unarmed, unsuspecting victim; no matter how good the other might be when using a revolver.

"He'll tell nobody!" Gilbertson screeched and sprang by Galbraith to launch a savage cut directed at the side of the small Texan's neck.

Shouting the threat merely served to increase Dusty's awareness of his peril. Watching the Volunteer, even while being addressed by Major Galbraith, Dusty had noticed the stealthy withdrawal of the sabre. Nor did the young Texan need to strain his brain to follow Gilbertson's line of reasoning.

What came as a surprise was the speed and precision of the Volunteer's attack. For once in his life, Dusty had come close to making the mistake of underestimating the potential of an enemy. Nothing he had seen of Gilbertson during their short acquaintance caused Dusty to form a high opinion of the other's military prowess. So the ability displayed by the Volunteer's attack was completely unexpected.

Two things saved Dusty as Gilbertson leapt forward in a *flèche* attack. He had observed the preparations for it and he knew enough about fencing to establish in what manner his assailant meant to strike. Held in supination, with the back of the hand pointing towards the ground, the sabre could only be used for a cut at the chest, abdomen, or side of the head. The second factor in saving Dusty was his own superb speed of reaction.

Knowing where the sabre was aimed, Dusty threw his left leg outwards and bent his right knee. Ducking his head and lowering his torso, he sank below the sweeping thirty-six inch long blade.

There had not been a moment to spare. So close did Gilbertson come to success that the edge of his blade sliced into the upper part of the campaign hat's crown and ripped it from Dusty's head. Throwing himself aside, Dusty landed erect and facing his assailant.

"Get set, Cap'n Dusty!" Surtees bellowed. "I'm com——"

"Stay back there!" Dusty answered.

If the Dragoons saw his companion charging forward, without being sure of why, they might open fire. That would end any hope of retrieving Gilbertson and making him pay for his treachery. Fortunately Surtees had been a soldier long enough to take even an unpalatable order; and possessed sufficient faith to figure his captain could get out of the present difficulty without requiring help. So he made no attempt to start the horses moving.

Crouching side by side on the rim above the camp, Kiowa and Prince had watched Gilbertson launch his treacherous attack. With a moaning splutter of invective, the young recruit snatched up Surtees' Enfield rifle and cradled the butt against his shoulder.

"Quit that!" ordered the sergeant, placing the palm of his left hand onto the rifle's hammer and preventing his companion from cocking it. "You know what we was told to do."

Before leaving the two soldiers, Dusty had given strict and definite orders. Under no circumstances were they to make their presence known to the Yankees. If the flag of truce should be violated, they must watch what happened; but remain concealed. Then they were to return at all speed and inform Ole Devil of Dusty's fate. Producing Dusty's gunbelt and Henry would be evidence that he had been unarmed at the time. The incident would be a powerful propaganda weapon for Ole Devil. So, much as doing it went against the grain, Kiowa aimed to carry out his captain's orders.

"The bastard'll kill Cap'n Fog!" Prince blazed, trying to tug the rifle free from Kiowa's grasp.

"Cap'n Dusty don't kill *that* easy," the sergeant answered. "Which you'd be's like to hit him as the Yankee from here, with a strange rifle. Look! That Dragoon major's taking cards."

"Gilbertson!" Galbraith bellowed, but he knew that no words could halt the wild-eyed, raging Volunteer.

Spluttering curses, Gilbertson charged at the unarmed Texan. Watching him draw near, Dusty noticed that the Volunteer's hand was no longer in supination.

He must mean to try for another target!

With the knuckles pointing downwards in pronation, any cut could best be directed to the opponent's flank.

So it proved. Around flashed the sabre, directed towards Dusty's ribs. A leap to the rear carried the small Texan clear, then a rapid crouch downwards followed by a bound to the right took him beyond the reach of the backhand chop that came after the cut had ended.

Galbraith's breath hissed through his teeth as he visualised the consequences of the treacherous attack. No matter how his people tried to hush it up, the story would come out. Very soon the whole world would know that a Yankee officer had broken his word and violated a flag of truce; and how an unarmed man had been vilely betrayed, then done to death.

The incident would reflect badly upon the integrity of the United States' Army; bring disrepute to the 6th "New Jersey" Dragoons; and be damning in the extreme to Major Galbraith himself as the senior officer present and the man who had accepted the correctly-requested call for a truce.

There could be only one answer.

Stop Gilbertson!

To hell with the influence the Volunteer's father might wield in New Hampstead, or in the Federal Congress. No matter how General Buller would react when learning of Galbraith's actions. Whatever happened as a result of it, Gilbertson must be prevented from committing a cold-blooded, dastardly murder.

Watching Dusty as he started to draw his sabre, Galbraith decided that the young Texan knew something of fencing. Both of his evasions had shown a knowledge of where the blows would be directed. Of course most wealthy young Southerners received instruction in handling sabre or *epee-de-combat*. Galbraith's every instinct told him that Captain Fog could hold his own against the Volunteer, given a chance to do so.

The problem facing Galbraith at that moment was how best to put Captain Fog in a position to defend himself.

Flashing across his right hand, the Dragoon slid his sabre from its sheath.

"Here, Captain Fog!" Galbraith yelled, spiking the point of the sabre into the ground and, springing aside, left the weapon standing erect. "Take this and defend yourself."

"Blast him!" Prince spat out, still trying to tear his rifle from Kiowa's grip, "that Yankee major sure ain't doing much."

Seeing the major's action, Gilbertson snarled and pressed forward his assault with vigour and determination. At Galbraith's words, Dusty flickered a glance by his attacker. Some distance separated the small Texan from the sword; which raised the question of how to reach it.

Returning his full attention to Gilbertson, Dusty sprang aside as the other rushed up. Although he did not like the idea, Dusty darted by the man and headed towards the Dragoon's sabre on the run. Swinging around, mouthing obscenities, Gilbertson gave chase. Striding out fast, the unencumbered Texan drew away from his assailant whose progress was not helped by slashing wicked cuts at his departing enemy.

Putting on a burst of speed, Dusty reached the sabre. Down stabbed his right hand in passing, entering the hilt and plucking the weapon from the ground. However, although armed, he did not halt and face the Volunteer immediately.

Known to its users by the unflattering sobriquet "The Old Wrist-Breaker," the Model of 1840 sabre—copied from the French Army's 1822 type—had been replaced in the Union Army by a lighter, slimmer-bladed variety in 1860. Following the lead of their Federal contemporaries, the Confederate arms manufacturers had produced the more easily-handled Model of 1860 pattern for their cav-

alry. Specially made for him by the company of L. Haiman
& Brother, Dusty's sabre was even lighter than the standard type. So he needed a brief respite to adjust to the
heavier weapon in his hand.

With the knucklebow of the guard hanging downwards,
Dusty gripped the front of the handle by the first joints of
the thumb and forefinger and curled the other fingers less
tightly about it. The weight of the sabre was mainly sup-
ported by the pommel-end of the handle pressing against
the heel of his palm. Held in such a manner, the hand could
be turned from pronation through the supination so as to
make the best use of the blade's cutting edge, the eight-
inch long false edge on the back, or the point.

Having obtained the necessary grip, Dusty thrust five
more long strides that pulled him clear of Gilbertson. Then
he brought himself to a turning halt and faced the Volunteer. Pointing his right foot in the fighting line towards his
attacker, Dusty turned his left toe outwards to stand on
parted, slightly bent legs. Keeping his trunk erect, he
tucked his left hand's thumb into his waistband. With his
point raised, adopting an on-guard position in *tierce,* he
waited for the Volunteer to reach him.

On the rim, Kiowa removed his hand from the Enfield
rifle. Grinning at Prince, the sergeant relaxed.

"Likely the major's done enough," the dark-faced Texan
drawled.

So swiftly had everything happened, that Dusty held the
sabre and prepared to engage Gilbertson before the majority of Troop "G" realised that something had gone wrong
with the parley. Then excited voices raised, drawing other
Dragoons' attention. Forgetting their duty, ignoring the
possibility of a Rebel cavalry force lurking ready to attack,
the enlisted men stood up to obtain a better view of the
fight. No less interested, the captain and two lieutenants

converged at the double on Galbraith.

"What the hell's happening, Tam?" demanded Captain Miller worriedly.

"Gilbertson wants to murder Captain Fog," the major answered, without taking his eyes from the combatants. "I just evened things up."

"But—But——!" Miller croaked.

"It's better this way," Galbraith stated and told his subordinates why Dusty had come and asked for the parley.

"The hell he did!" Miller spat as he heard of Gilbertson's escape. Although he shared with his superior a repugnance for the Volunteer's behaviour, he felt that he should say something more. "Are you letting this go through all the way?"

"Right to the end, Fred."

"If Gilbertson loses——"

"I think that Captain Fog won't take the matter further."

"And if he wins?"

"That's what I'm counting on *not* happening, Fred," Galbraith admitted frankly.

Miller watched Dusty and Gilbertson, wishing that he could share his commanding officer's optimism. From what the captain could see, the issue was still very much in doubt.

Without hesitation, probably because he could not stop himself in time, Gilbertson plunged towards the small Texan. Counting on his extra reach, weight and strength, the Volunteer delivered a barrage of slashes and cuts that kept Dusty on the defensive for almost a minute. Trying no such refinements as thrusts, feints or lunges, Gilbertson continued to expend his energy in a hurricane assault of orthodox speed and force.

For his part, Dusty concentrated on following Beau Amesley's often-repeated advice to let the eye and the feet save the arm. The weapon he held was longer and heavier than the one to which he had become accustomed, so he used the passing seconds in gaining its feel, hang and balance.

Satisfied at last that he knew the sabre, Dusty changed his tactics and took the offensive. Like a rubber ball rebounding after being thrown at a wall, Gilbertson went into a retreat. Forced to withdraw and parry desperately, he rapidly lost the ground gained during his abortive whirlwind, carpet-beating assault. With growing anxiety, the Volunteer began to admit that he might be facing a man approaching his own skill. Gradually, however, he was compelled to swallow his bigoted pride and accept that once again a Rebel was proving superior to him.

"There," Kiowa said in satisfaction, watching Gilbertson being forced to give ground. "I told you there wasn't nothing to worry over."

"You told me," agreed Prince. "Only one thing worries me now."

"What'd that be?"

"What'll happen after Cap'n Dusty's licked that Yankee son-of-a-bitch?"

That point had also occurred to Kiowa, but he did not mention the matter to his companion.

Dusty originated another attack, bounding forward with his blade in pronation as it went for a cut to flank. Down dropped Gilbertson's point, executing a parry in low *tierce*. Falling back a little, with his blade held ready for a lunge, Dusty decided that the Volunteer intended to follow up the parry with a cut at his arm. When the blow came, Dusty made a parry in *seconde* and raised the attacking weapon. With his opponent's blade taken out of line, Dusty disengaged it and brought off a rapid cut to the head.

Seeing the danger, Gilbertson spread apart and bent his

knees, to duck beneath the arc of Dusty's blow. From the position he had gained, the Volunteer could have legitimately cut at Dusty's chest or abdomen. Instead, while still crouching, he swept his sabre around in an attempt to strike the small Texan's legs.

A low, angry mutter rose from the Dragoon officers, for such a tactic was regarded as a deliberate foul in a fencing match or during a serious duel. However, they saw that Dusty was aware of the danger and did not intervene.

Realising that he dealt with a man to whom honour, ethics and fair play had no meaning, Dusty had watched for and been ready to counter Gilbertson's foul manoeuvre. Bounding into the air, bending his knees and tucking his feet beneath him, he passed over the Volunteer's sabre.

On landing, Dusty stumbled slightly. Not sufficiently to throw him off his balance, but enough to make his sabre waver from its hitherto near-perfect guard. Thrusting up from his crouch, Gilbertson brought around his own weapon in a savage inwards beat and tried for a *sforzo* disarmament. Using his extra weight, the Volunteer struck the side of Dusty's blade with considerable force. Gilbertson hoped that the impact would so loosen the small Texan's hand on the hilt that he would lose his hold of it and he would be unable to parry the coming lunge or cut.

Although Dusty's strength and control prevented the former from happening, he could not stop his blade being forced to his attacker's left. Carried forward by his impetus, Gilbertson found himself approaching a position of *corps-a-corps*. Before the sabres' hilts met and their users halted chest to chest, the Volunteer saw a chance offered. Prompted by his fear of defeat, he took it. Bringing his left hand from his hip, he caught hold of the back of Dusty's blade. Keeping his fingers extended, to avoid the cutting edge, Gilbertson prepared to take advantage of his latest piece of foul play. Up swung his sabre, ready to smash the iron knucklebow of the guard into the Texan's face.

Once again Dusty's lightning fast reactions saved him. Feeling his blade gripped and immobilised, he guessed what Gilbertson intended to do even before the other's right hand began to lift. This latest attempt at foul play warned Dusty that he could not treat the Volunteer as an honourable enemy and so must fight fire with fire.

With Dusty Fog, to think was to act.

Up rose the small Texan's right foot, then drove down to smash the heel of his boot against the top of Gilbertson's forward instep. Pain caused the Volunteer to yelp, flinch and relax his grasp on Dusty's sabre. Oblivious of the furious shouts that rose from behind him, Dusty rotated his wrist to the left almost 90°. By tugging back on the hilt, he drew the cutting edge across Gilbertson's involuntarily clutching fingers. Again the Volunteer cried out, even louder, as the edge bit into his phalanges. Jerking his hand from Dusty's weapon, he took a long stride to the rear. Doing so caused his down-driving hand to miss.

Having set his sabre free, Dusty also started to withdraw. The knucklebow of the Volunteer's weapon almost grazed Dusty's face in passing, but it failed to strike him.

In a flash, the small Texan retaliated. With his hand in supination, he propelled his blade around to pass over Gilbertson's left shoulder. Slicing into the side of the Volunteer's neck, the sabre almost removed his head from his shoulders. Throwing his weapon aside, the man spun around and went down. He landed on his back spreadeagled and lifeless.

Sucking in deep breaths, Dusty stepped back and lowered his borrowed sabre. He saw Surtees galloping towards him and heard the Dragoon officers running in his direction. Turning to the latter, he felt puzzled by the anger and disapproval they displayed. Then he realised what had caused the emotions. The Dragoons had been unable to see the reason for Dusty's apparently unsporting action.

"Look at his left hand, Major," Dusty suggested before any word of condemnation could be directed at him.

Striding by the small Texan, Galbraith knelt at Gilbertson's side. One glance informed the Dragoon that nothing could save the Volunteer's life. In a way that was all to the good. Unless Captain Fog insisted on making the deplorable incident public, the affair could be kept a secret. Talking about it would do more harm than good.

Having reached that conclusion, the major took up the Volunteer's limp left hand. He looked for a moment at the bloody gash across the fingers and nodded his understanding. Satisfied, he came to his feet and faced his subordinates.

"He grabbed Captain Fog's blade," Galbraith announced.

"It wasn't his first foul trick," Captain Miller went on coldly. "I don't blame you for playing him at his own game, Captain Fog."

A mutter of agreement rose from the two lieutenants. Gathering a handful of grass, Dusty cleaned the sabre's blade. With that done, he reversed the weapon and held its hilt towards Galbraith.

"My thanks, sir," Dusty said.

"I suppose that I shouldn't have let you fight him," Galbraith admitted as he returned his sabre to its sheath. Then he stiffened and growled, "The hell I shouldn't. He deserved all he got and I don't regret him getting it."

"Comes to that, sir," Dusty answered ruefully, "I shouldn't've killed him. Like I told you, he was due to be exchanged for one of our captains this morning."

Looking at the small Texan—although he would never

again think of Dusty Fog as being small—Galbraith saw the other's predicament. By a convention of war, a prisoner could be exchanged for a man of equal rank held by the opposition. However, Captain Fog no longer had a prisoner to offer in exchange. Another convention of war was that an officer's word must be his bond. Gilbertson had admitted to giving his parole with the full intention of breaking it. If he had lived, he would have been handed back to his escort.

Any way that Major Galbraith looked at the problem, he saw only one honourable solution. The Army of the United States must uphold its obligations and preserve the conventions of war.

"As far as I'm concerned, Captain Fog," the Dragoons' major said soberly. "You delivered Gilbertson alive and in good health. If you'll accompany me to the Snake Ford, I'll guarantee your officer is released in exchange for him."